For more than forty years,
Yearling has been the leading name
in classic and award-winning literature
for young readers.

Yearling books feature children's
favorite authors and characters,
providing dynamic stories of adventure,
humor, history, mystery, and fantasy.

Trust Yearling paperbacks to entertain,
inspire, and promote the love of reading
in all children.

AUDREY COULOUMBIS

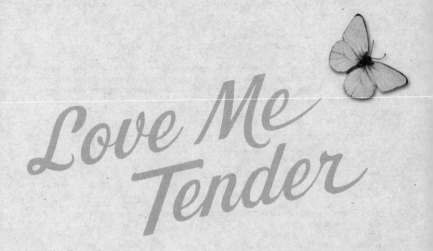

Love Me Tender

A YEARLING BOOK

Published by Yearling
an imprint of Random House Children's Books
a division of Random House, Inc., New York

This is a work of fiction. Names, characters, places, and incidents either are the product of the author's imagination or are used fictitiously. Any resemblance to actual persons, living or dead, events, or locales is entirely coincidental.

Visit us on the Web! www.randomhouse.com/kids

Educators and librarians, for a variety of teaching tools, visit us at
www.randomhouse.com/teachers

The Library of Congress has cataloged the hardcover edition of this work as follows:
Couloumbis, Audrey.
Love me tender / by Audrey Couloumbis.
p. cm
Summary: Thirteen-year-old Elvira worries about her future when, after a fight, her father heads to Las Vegas for an Elvis impersonator competition and her pregnant mother takes her and her younger sister to Memphis to visit a grandmother the girls have never met.
ISBN 978-0-375-83839-2 (trade) — ISBN 978-0-375-93839-9 (lib. bdg.)
[1. Family problems—Fiction. 2. Pregnancy—Fiction. 3. Elvis Presley impersonators—Fiction.] I. Title.
PZ7.C8305Lov 2008   [Fic]—dc22   2006033162

ISBN 978-0-375-83840-8 (pbk.)

Reprinted by arrangement with Random House Books for Young Readers

Printed in the United States of America

April 2009

10 9 8 7 6 5 4 3 2 1

First Yearling Edition

For my daughter,
Nikki,
protector of rabbits
and loved ones

Love Me Tender

Chapter 1

EARLY FRIDAY afternoon, Daddy left mad.

He carried his guitar. The weather had turned so hot, the sweaty circles on his T-shirt looked like the wings of an insect against his back.

I followed him, dragging his duffel and panting. "Daddy, this thing is too heavy. What all are you carrying in here?"

What, besides his blue suede shoes and tight white jeans, did he need?

"Stuff," he said, and kept on going.

Okay, he needed a round brush and his diffuser and this tube of hair gunk he called "the genuine article." He'd dyed his honey-colored hair so black it made me think of fur, only I couldn't name an animal that would gleam navy blue in the sunlight, coated in Brylcreem.

Daddy always walked with a swagger as soon as he combed his hair in this rolled-over way. But this time it was a fast ticked-off swagger; I had to move it to make the driveway with any time to spare for questions.

I only had one: You're coming back, aren't you? Only I couldn't get up the nerve to ask.

I let the duffel drop next to his feet. He'd hung his white Elvis jacket from a curtain rod installed in the cab of his pickup truck. I saw a yellow butterfly had been trapped inside, drawn to the little rainbows bouncing off the shiny sequins.

That butterfly clamped itself to the back of Daddy's shoulder as he set his guitar case into the leg space of the passenger seat. He took no notice, saying, "I'm relying on you, Elvira."

"Me?" I lost my breath a little bit.

He threw the duffel into the back of the truck. He said, "Don't let things fall apart once I'm gone."

"Like what?"

Daddy looked like he shouldn't have to tell me. He went around and got into the truck. That yellow butterfly was blown off a ways as the truck started up, then came back to flutter around like it was lost. I watched Daddy till he turned the corner, taking the back road out to the airport.

Now my breath came too fast. What did he expect me to do?

I went back into the house.

The minute Daddy started packing, Mel, my mother, took to the recliner like soap to a sponge. She hadn't moved. I said to her, "He would have taken you along if he could."

"He could have taken me if he wanted me along," she said. Her straight dark hair had been twisted up off her neck while I was out there with Daddy, and the ends stuck up at the back of her head like the bristles of a broom.

"Okay, but then we'd've *all* had to go. By car. Lots more luggage, and about a million bathroom stops." She shot me a dirty look. "For Kerrie, of course," I added, but I'd been thinking about this. If this was Daddy's logic, it was, well, logical.

"I took care of my little sister when I was thirteen," Mel said.

"That was in the Dark Ages," I said. "There are laws against abandoning your children now."

"My folks went out of state to a funeral," she said, her eyes on the TV screen. "They left me in charge."

"That was more in the nature of an emergency, I guess."

"Miss Nelda would look in on you."

My eyes went wide. "She uses a walker. You can't expect her to jog over here every couple of hours."

"Okay, then. You could report to her."

"You don't mean that," I said, wondering how else to reply to a woman who had recently turned into a walking time bomb. "If you did, you'd have said it before Daddy left."

There were gunshots on TV.

Mel settled more deeply into the recliner. She's a movie

3

junkie—that's what Daddy calls her, anyway, when she shells out for extra movie channels. Personally, I never thought this was a bad trait in a mother, just I had never seen the junkie part take such hold of her.

"I hope I don't have to tell you not to mention this idea to Kerrie," I said. "She'll have to be peeled off you like a Band-Aid for days. Weeks, even."

My sister, Kerrie, had recently turned eight, but she'd started behaving like she was three again. She wasn't the only one. "I hate it when you stop talking to me in the middle of a conversation," I said.

"I know." She flipped the channel.

Mel was not herself, I could see that. But she was not herself in the worst possible way. If she got tired in the middle of the railroad tracks and lay down to take a nap, wouldn't she get up if she heard the train whistle?

"You're really annoying me," I said.

"I know," we both said at the same time, and I left the room. I didn't know who to be mad at first: Daddy, who'd chugged off without so much as a wave good-bye, or Mel, who'd sent him away mad.

Daddy had entered a competition—he didn't like for us to call it a contest. He explained how the words make people feel. The person in a contest is a contestant, one of many trying to win, and the whole feel of the word is weak. But competitions are all about competency, and competence is strength.

The Elvis Bake-Off, that's what Mel called it, and

anyone with half a brain would pack up and go after she ridiculed their competition that way. Daddy went out the door, singing, "You ain't nothin' but a hound dog, a-cryin' all the time."

We all knew the next line: *Well, you ain't never caught a rabbit and you ain't no friend of mine.* The song echoed through my mind, over and over. I looked in on Kerrie, who was sitting in the middle of Mel and Daddy's bed.

There was stuff tossed all over the room, partly the usual mess of closets too small to hold everything, partly Daddy's packing mess. Kerrie added to it with a lot of cut-up newspaper.

She'd been trying for days to master the art of folding paper and cutting it to get connected paper dolls. She was sometimes successful enough to try it on white paper, but then she'd mess up again.

"I've got it," she said, unfolding her latest effort. They connected at the toes, but not at the hands. She wasn't using newspaper.

"What kind of paper is that?"

"Sheet music," she said. "But old stuff."

"All of Daddy's stuff is old."

"He said I could have it."

I looked at the paper dolls. "You should stick to news-paper a little while longer."

At hour four, after the third movie started, I heated boil-in bags of creamed spinach and buttered shoepeg corn. It was too hot to bother with anything else.

Kerrie, with some of Daddy's pink sponge rollers flopping around her face, begged for cheese macaroni. I guarantee if I had started out to make cheese macaroni, she'd have pined for creamed spinach.

I served Mel's meal on a tray, like she was ill. "Elvira?" she said, like it would be anybody else. "Would you adjust the bright?"

She acted like she didn't even notice the food. Only, when I came back for the tray, the plate looked clean enough to get by without washing it. "Are you getting up soon?" I asked her.

"I just need ten minutes alone," she said, like we'd been badgering her for her opinions on how to end world famine or something. Actually, she said those words about a million times a week.

"When your ten minutes are up, it's Kerrie's bath time, and she doesn't listen to me unless I'm holding out a Popsicle."

"So give her a Popsicle."

I hate my family.

I know that's supposed to happen when you turn thirteen, but a year ago I would have said it's not going to happen to me. I loved Mel and Daddy. Not that they looked perfect to me. I mean, they didn't look perfect to anybody, I'm sure.

Daddy hardly ever talked sports or politics. Instead, he kept an elderly car in mint condition. He stocked his jukebox. If he had a day off, he drove all over to flea markets in search of records. And he looked at gardens. Every so often, he was asked to do his Elvis thing at an anniversary party.

Mel bought falling-apart furniture at auctions and fixed it up to look almost new. This was more comfortable and less embarrassing to live with than it sounds. Most of my friends think anything made of "real wood" means it's an antique. As for Daddy, they only thought he was weird until they heard him sing.

It's like my parents got infected with a virus that made them love anything old and secondhand. They could've gone on this way forever with no complaint from me. Only, in this past year, my feet went from size six to size nine.

I had this in common with my mother, and I was not in the mood to forgive. Neither was she. "Don't think shoes and bras are cheap. Try to wear something out."

My sister said, "Can I have the sneakers you painted?"

I had my doubts about her too. "Because they're old and secondhand?"

"Because I like them."

"They're yours, I guess."

I also shot up four inches, making me the tallest girl, not just in my class but in the whole next grade. I "developed." That's how they put it in health class. Kindly.

Daddy started worrying about how my clothes fit. Basically, he wanted me to wear a tent. And when I didn't want to wear a tent, he said to Mel, "Next thing you know, she'll be coming home with a tattoo on her behind or a ring in her navel."

I said, "That is just uncalled-for."

"Maybe so," he said. "But I don't want my daughter looking like she bears a factory stamp or perforations of the kind seen on a ticket stub."

"How about if I stick a record label on my forehead," I said. "Would that be okay with you?"

He sent me to my room, which really wasn't fair. I had been explaining my parents' weirdnesses to my friends for a long time; it wasn't my job to make sure I kept fitting the box I came in.

The thing is, I never expected Mel and Daddy to wake up on my thirteenth birthday sounding as dated as their furniture and music. I thought they were going to be the cool parents.

I think even they thought they were going to be cool.

During the same year, Mel got pregnant.

Chapter 2

THE SAME day Mel found out she was pregnant, Daddy lost three of his best landscaping customers. All of them with special gardens Daddy had created. One had been photographed for a national magazine. It put New Hope, North Carolina, on the map.

The other two got featured every year as "Garden of the Month." The local garden club stuck big signs on their lawns. They owed Daddy, all three, for getting them talked about around town in the nicest way.

Their reason for firing Daddy? So they could hire a company that was going to charge them less to manage their outstanding yards. Mel knew about it right away, since she took the calls.

All Kerrie and I knew was, when we got home from

school, the mood was not good. We spread peanut butter on saltines. We stood in the kitchen to eat them while Daddy painted an arbor he'd built over the back door.

I heard him say to Mel, "Sometimes I wonder if I'm anybody special anymore. I think I'd be invisible if I got up on a real stage."

I thought, Poor Daddy.

"Why, of course you wouldn't be invisible," Mel said in an annoyed tone. She'd had a hard day too, and Daddy didn't know the half of it. None of us did. She said, "You'd have that guitar, those tight jeans, the hair. No one could miss that hair."

"Jeez, Mel," Daddy said.

But when she spoke again, she was gentler. "Then, when you sing, there's his voice."

Daddy said, "Thanks, Mel. You always know how to make me feel better." But only a few minutes later, he didn't take the news of her hard day nearly as well.

"I went to the doctor for my regular checkup and got a little surprise," Mel said. "I'm a month on the way."

There was a silence during which I didn't know what this meant. I thought maybe even Daddy didn't know what she meant. But then he did.

"I don't understand," Daddy said, as if she had shown him a dog turd in his slipper. "You told me you were done when Kerrie was born."

"I didn't say I *tried* to get pregnant," Mel said. Shouted. More quietly, she said, "I didn't choose this."

"Well, I didn't choose this either." A moment later, Daddy added, "I didn't mean that the way it sounded."

But from that point to this, things were not good.

Mel's mood slid up and down like notes on a musical scale. She stopped liking real food and didn't want to cook it. She ate so many blue Popsicles, it looked like she was using food coloring for lipstick.

Otherwise, Mel being pregnant didn't make much of an impression on anyone but Mel, and sad to say, sometimes I thought she was making it up. Once, I told her I thought she was just getting fat.

She ran into the bathroom and cried. I knocked and told her I didn't mean it. She wouldn't open up, not even for Daddy, when he stood outside the door and sang, "You ain't nothin' but a hound dog, a-cryin' all the time."

It might not have been a wise choice. We had to go across the street to Miss Nelda to use the bathroom that night.

Inside of three months, Daddy got all his customers back without even trying. It took some time and a lot of weeding, but we all worked together to shape up those gardens again. Still, something had changed. Daddy stopped looking for records and spent more time in the basement playing his guitar.

Not a month later, there came the flea fiasco. That's what Mel called it, trying to make it sound cute for one of the garden club ladies. Later on, Daddy called it "the weekend you hacked up the dog."

It did tend to lose cuteness when put just that way.

It was a weekend gone wrong. Mel was mad before Daddy went off Friday evening with some of his buddies. We didn't have other plans or anything. Mel wouldn't usually care if Daddy went or that she didn't or even that he wasn't coming home till Sunday night. Only, Mel took the call, and the fellow who invited Daddy said to her, "No wimmin allowed."

"What is the point he's trying to make? 'No wimmin allowed,'" she kept saying to Daddy, imitating the way his friend had said it. "I can't believe he said that to me. I'm the mother of your children."

It was clear to me Mel expected Daddy to say he wasn't interested in going. It was not that clear to Daddy. He said to her, "Don't take it personally" and "It's just us men and our guitars at a cabin in the woods, that's all he meant."

"Just us min and our geetars?" Mel said, in exactly the same way she'd been saying, "No wimmin allowed."

Daddy went anyway. He didn't take our basset hound, but not because he was mad. What he said was, "Hound's just going to pick up more fleas out there in the woods, and he's crazy with them already."

So really, the shave was practically Daddy's idea.

After he left, Mel said, "The only sure way to get rid of fleas is to take away their hiding place," and shaved off Hound's fur with an electric clippers. Or as much of it as she could before he made his escape.

Really, Hound stood still for it while she worked on his sides and belly, where the fleas got at him most often. He didn't appear to mind having a naked pink rat's tail either.

He stood the way he always did, with front feet pointed out, as if he couldn't make up his mind which way to go.

Hound appeared to have taken an interest in our opinion of the job Mel did, which is where our dog always stood out from other hounds. He was not just a sad face, he had smarts. He liked to follow the progress of practically anything going on—in this case, his shave.

But when Mel ran the clippers between his ears and down the long bridge of his nose, he took off like he'd heard a dinner call down the street, ears a-flapping.

We looked all around the neighborhood for him.

Mel said, "I thought he was liking it."

"It probably sounded like a dentist's drill in Hound's brain," I said. "*Brzzz,* all over his face."

Mel started to cry. It used to be that crying was not at all like her. But her hormones acted pretty much like the fleas on the dog. They made her crazy.

I said, "Really, Daddy has to know you were only trying to help."

That's when Mel started calling him "your daddy's dog." At first, this sounded kind of cool, like Hound had been promoted to more than just a family dog. Only later did I see that it warned of the storm to come.

We borrowed Miss Nelda's car—in case we found Hound and wanted to give him a ride home. We couldn't put him in Daddy's car. Even Kerrie and I sat on blankets in the car so shoe buckles or a zipper pull wouldn't scratch the leather. It's mint. Dog toenails could not touch that leather.

We drove further than we could've walked, calling out the windows and watching down driveways for him. Mel told me Hound was a four-month-old puppy when she met Daddy. She pounded the palm of her hand on the steering wheel, telling me. Hormones.

"He's even older than I thought," I said as we stopped for a red light. Mel let her forehead rest on the steering wheel. I tried to lighten the mood. "Hound will be home when we get there. He'll have called out for pizza."

"Your daddy has loved that dog longer than he has loved any of us." This without lifting her head.

"Green light."

Mel pulled herself together and continued driving. She said, "This is the stuff of lifelong grudges, Elvira. If I don't get that dog back, your daddy and I have turned a corner."

"Don't let's go off the deep end," I said. It was something my friend Debs's mother said pretty often, helpfully, since she's a family therapist. I thought it might help Mel.

"Elvira, if you say that to me again, I'll put you right out of the car and you'll have to walk home."

"Then you'd have to explain to Daddy how you lost me too."

She pulled over to the side of the road so fast Kerrie shouted from the backseat, "Hey! This is how people get whiplash."

"You too, smarty-pants," Mel said to Kerrie. "Out."

"We'll write when we find jobs," I said once we were standing on the curb. Mel drove a block and a half, then pulled over again to wait. She had the nerve to honk twice to hurry us along.

Kerrie and I took our time getting to the car, calling Hound.

Some hours later and still no Hound in sight, Mel panicked and called the animal shelter to see if he'd been picked up. He hadn't. "Well, can you keep an eye out for him? It's my husband's dog," Mel said to the person on the phone, and started to cry again. "I will just have to kill myself if I've gone and lost him over a few fleas."

They gave her a hotline number that she called, thinking it was another shelter. It turned out to be a crisis center where they pretty much talk people out of jumping off buildings.

"I'll save this number for your daddy," Mel said.

One of Daddy's customers called the next day, practically the minute after Daddy got home, to say our dog was hiding behind her garden shed. She believed Hound had been the victim of a joke, that somebody's kids were let to run wild with dog clippers.

Hound died in his sleep that very night. He was old, and maybe running around the neighborhood hadn't done him any good. But it wasn't Mel's fault, even Daddy said so.

Mel said she would always feel guilty, but maybe after a while she'd stop feeling like she had to scrub her skin with Brillo pads to take her mind off it.

It was a rough weekend, but I thought that was likely to be the end of it.

I was wrong.

Chapter 3

OVER SUPPER one night, Daddy made an announcement. "There's an important competition coming up, and I'm taking part in it."

Mel had lately gone from morning sickness to evening backache, but she took this well enough. "What kind of garden do we need to grow?"

"Not gardens," Daddy said. "I'm making a comeback."

"A comeback?" This was Kerrie, who didn't know the word.

"Your daddy's going to be the King this year," Daddy said, which only caused Kerrie to get that crease between her eyebrows. "I have to go pick my music."

"Mel?" I said after he'd gone down to the cellar.

"Don't ask me," she said. And then added, "I think I'm

having a nightmare." She followed him downstairs, where they had a long argument.

Partly it was about Mel wanting Daddy to stay home. And then it was about how Daddy didn't want us to go along. The upshot was, having another baby didn't fit in with Daddy's plans to make a big comeback out there in Las Vegas.

Kerrie was lying awake in the dark when I went to bed later on that evening. She didn't sound babyish, she didn't even sound like an eight-year-old, when she asked me, "Do you think they're going to get a divorce?"

Kerrie could deal with anything when she was using this voice. When she was four, she told me I didn't have to pretend about Santa Claus unless Mel and Daddy were in the room. When I asked why didn't she tell Mel and Daddy she knew, she said they gave better presents when they were pretending.

But now we were talking about divorce. Kerrie could probably handle it, but I wasn't ready to admit how worried I was. I said, "Mel isn't going to let Daddy off that easily."

"It could have a good side to it," Kerrie said. "We'd be just like all the other kids."

Kerrie and I were practically the only kids we knew who had a full set of parents that had never been married to anybody else. I said, "Divorce won't make us happy."

"Marietta's mother said it made her happy."

"That's because Marietta's mother was unhappy before the divorce. Mel and Daddy were happy. Are happy. They've just forgotten it for a little while."

"It's been a long time."

"The important thing to remember is, it's not about them, not really." I had talked it out with Debs. Her mom, too. "This is all about gardens. And customers. It's about business."

"I'm not going to have any of those things when I grow up."

"Probably a good idea."

"Good night, Elvira."

I turned out the reading light, thinking it was about Daddy feeling appreciated by his customers. Or by an audience. Or by us. I hoped *Mel* got that.

Then the baby started to kick.

Babies should kick, Mel told us when at first only she could feel it. Then, once we *could* feel the baby kick, Mel kept making us hold a hand to her basketball of a belly and go, "Oh, wow."

It creeped me out.

Last year, in science class, we watched this film on the daily life of insect larvae. The way those worms looked, that's how it felt to have that baby rub up against me from the other side of my mother's skin.

Late in July, Mel threw herself a "seventh-month party." She printed invitations and let us find them on the table one morning. After blank looks all around, Daddy gave Kerrie and me five dollars. "Walk down to the drugstore and get her a present," he said. "Get her bath gel or something."

We bought a tin wind chime and a scented candle.

Mel opened her presents, saying, "Oh, you shouldn't

have" and "This is lovely." Daddy gave her a vintage T-shirt that read IF YOU CHOKE A SMURF, WHAT COLOR WILL IT TURN? Mel said, "Isn't this fun?"

She looked like a snake that swallowed an egg when she tried it on, and they had to explain to Kerrie that a Smurf was a cartoon character, a little blue man. So if he was already blue, blah-blah-blah. Personally, I thought Daddy should have stuck to the bath gel idea.

We all enjoyed the chocolate ice cream cake. While Kerrie and I did the dishes, Mel ate another slice. She took a third slice into the living room to watch TV. She was finishing it off as Kerrie and I went to bed.

"That was strange," Kerrie whispered.

I shrugged.

I didn't think it was strange for Mel to give herself a little party. I was only surprised she invited us.

A week after that, the Belly just inflated, like a beach ball. Mel got so awkward, I kept making these stupid gallant gestures, like changing the lightbulb in the kitchen and cleaning the bathtub. Walking down to the Shop and Gas to buy her another box of Popsicles to satisfy her cravings for blue food coloring.

I was disgusting, but I couldn't help myself. I felt sorry for her.

Watching my sister stir her buttered corn into her spinach, I wondered why I used to think all my problems would be over once I grew up.

Kerrie said, "Why are you looking at me like that?"

I said, "Don't stir your food together. It looks disgusting, like mashed sweet peas."

"What's disgusting about that?"

"Mel will be buying baby food pretty soon," I said. "You'll have a chance to find out."

While Mel watched TV, on and on, she ignored us entirely. We could be in the same room, that was okay; we could watch the movie, okay too. But we couldn't ask her for anything. We couldn't touch her, even. She flicked us off like houseflies.

Kerrie brought out the deck of cards. "Play with us, Mel," I said. "We need three for Hearts."

"I just don't have the energy," she said. I hated to hear her say that, because it made me feel like I sort of didn't have the energy either.

"Then it's War," I said to Kerrie, who didn't look especially disappointed. She wins at War more often than at Hearts, sad to say.

A little before midnight, Mel said, "Pop up some corn, Elvira, why don't you?"

"Because I'm tired, that's why."

Like someone lying on her deathbed, Mel said, "I have a craving for popcorn," and I acted like I didn't hear her. After about twenty minutes, she scraped up enough energy to pop corn and gave us, Kerrie and me, each a cereal bowl full. Mel filled a big wooden salad bowl for herself.

There was something horrible about not being given a fair share. Kerrie and I gobbled as if we were in a race to the finish. Then Kerrie said, "I want more," and reached to scoop some out of the salad bowl.

"Get Elvira to make you some," Mel said, pushing my sister's hand away.

I hated Mel so much right then, burning tears came to my eyes. "I won't either. It's too much trouble to go to." Then I thought of how to get a rise out of her. Mel didn't trust nonstick coatings, pressure cookers, toaster ovens, and most of all, microwave ovens.

I said, "If we had a microwave, Kerrie could do her own. I don't see why we can't even have a microwave." Normally, this would be the start of the big lecture on how early microwave users cooked their very bones, reaching in and out of those invisible rays.

Normally, Mel would tell us microwave doors are not even solid but are a grid of pinholes the rays can shoot through, starting cancers in the breasts and bellies of women who are standing impatiently in front of them, tapping their French-painted toes.

These were not normal times. Mel said, "I'll think about it."

By midnight, Mel was watching a movie about a lonely housewife who follows some woman she read about in the personal ads until she ends up living the other woman's life. It might've been scary to think Mel felt like following somebody into another life, but the way she had folded herself into the recliner, I figured she was going to be there the rest of her life.

The rest of mine.

We were all up way past my bratty sister's bedtime. When Kerrie roused herself enough to notice Mel had eaten the last of the chocolate chip cookies, she threw herself onto the floor in a tantrum, kicking one foot so her body hitched around and around like a balky carousel.

This was something she had outgrown once. When she was little, the only way to deal with her was to pick her up off the floor at the supermarket or the toy store and carry her out to the car, kicking and screaming. I didn't have to be the momma to know that we had to nip this silliness in the bud.

But Mel and Daddy had made up their minds to ignore her babyish behavior, which meant I had to live with it too.

Mel said, "Take care of your sister."

I went to bed with a Save the Earth chocolate bar and a nice thick book. I played an old concert tape from Daddy's stash. The applause after every song just made me feel like, somewhere in the world, people were having a good time.

About an hour later, my sister climbed into my bed and curled up like a cat against my leg. Her nose had stuffed up, her eyes were red-rimmed, her sponge curlers gone.

"How long is this going to go on?" Kerrie asked.

"How long is what going to go on?"

"Pregnancy."

"Two more months." I hoped my thick book would last

me that long. The chocolate was already gone. "And then there's the baby."

A whiny moan was Kerrie's only response.

I was tempted to make her get into her own bed, but with Mel acting like we didn't exist, I couldn't do it. So I let Kerrie stay, let her fall asleep next to me. I even trailed my fingers through her rumpled hair a few times to soothe her.

Even though I hated her too.

Chapter 4

WHEN I got out of bed the next morning, Mel was sleeping through a noisy car chase. She hadn't moved off the recliner for seventeen hours straight, except to go to the bathroom.

How do I know?

The toilet is on the other side of the wall from my bed. I could hear it flush every hour and a half, when a movie ended. Mel never bothered to turn the sound down one bit all night long either.

I turned the TV off.

It was past two in the afternoon when she got up, looking like a bear coming out of a winter-long hibernation. I saw this out of the corners of my eyes, because I didn't look up from my book.

Kerrie was out, riding her bike around and around the

block. I'd told her not to cross the street, to keep an eye on the driveways, and to stay off people's flower beds. But when Mel came out of the bathroom and asked, "Where is your sister," I only shrugged.

Mel went to look through the screen door. "Does that mean you honestly have no idea?"

I didn't answer. While Mel slept, whether I wanted to or not, I had to feed and generally supervise my sister. Mel was not forgiven.

She stepped out on the porch and shouted Kerrie's name.

After two more yells, with a waiting pause to follow, Mel turned to me and said, "If you'd watched her like I tell you to, everything would be fine."

"I. Don't. Think. So." I made each word an arrow I hoped would pierce her heart.

"Tell me you know where that child is."

How could I know? Kerrie could be on any one of four sides of the block. Or the monster under the bed could have eaten her.

That's what I wished for during the first five months of her life, when she lived in the ruffled lace bassinet. I had squirted trails of dripping formula from the bed to the bassinet, all the while saying in a coaxing voice, "This way to the tender little baby." I did this maybe five or six times before Mel caught me at it. That's when I learned the monster didn't live under the bed.

I said, "She's not my job, she's yours, and I won't do it anymore."

Mel snatched up the telephone and punched at some numbers. "This is Melisand-silent-*e* Ruggiero, and I want to report a missing child." She spelled her whole name, as she always has to, and told them where we live.

I kept shut. This was even better than I could have hoped for.

Mel went on to give the police a description of Kerrie. "What was she wearing?" Mel asked, turning to me.

I gave her back a blank stare.

"Shorts and a top," Mel answered, as if she actually knew. "I'm such a wreck, I've forgotten the colors."

This was a guess, and it was a wrong guess. Kerrie was wearing a dark blue skinny-knit dress at least one size too small and a pair of orange tights with a hole in one knee. I had nothing to do with these choices.

There were more questions, and finally some kind of finish to the conversation that I couldn't hear. "If anything's happened to her, it will be your fault," Mel said as she hung up.

"I would agree with you if I was her mother, but I'm not," I said. "I have a feeling the police are going to see it my way."

"Go to your room."

"I better wait, in case they need to question me."

"You'd better get out of here before I give in to the urge to do you mortal damage. It would be satisfying for me, but just too painful for your daddy to come home to."

I slouched away with a dramatic sigh, holding hidden

in my heart the joy of hearing the words "for your daddy to come home to."

Once in my room, I slammed the door hard enough to shiver the rafters. Then I lickety-split locked it, because in one second flat Mel was banging on my door to beat all saints.

I didn't wait to see if she would kick it in with her number nines but flicked on my sound system, turned the volume to high, then turned and jumped out of my window and into the flower bed.

Fat buds that would have been yellow daylilies in another few days rained on the ground. I crushed entire plants as I bounded through them in clumpy running shoes to escape certain death. I pictured myself as some cartoon giant flattening cities beneath my feet.

I leaped over the ridiculous twenty-four-inch picket fence in a single bound—laughing, I admit it—and cut through the neighboring backyard to complete my escape. Mel was peeved, really peeved. It might be days before she could give herself over to falling apart again.

I ran into Kerrie on my way to the candy store and told her she probably ought to go into hiding, the police were looking for her.

"What for?" she asked, straddling her bike. She looked awfully hot.

"They want you for murder. I'd hide out if I were you. The police don't listen to reason when they're after a killer."

"I didn't kill anyone," she said, her spiky hair standing up not only from sweat now, but from fear.

"They don't know that, that's the thing."

"I'll go over to—"

"Don't tell me," I yelled, putting my hands over my ears. "What if they try to wring it out of me?"

"You're right," she said. "You better get away from me so you can't be suspected too." And she rode away, fast.

I bought two Baby Ruth candy bars, three packages of peanut M&M's, and a bottle of iced tea to wash it all down. I felt a little bit bad about Kerrie.

Not because she is only eight years old, facing a life of hiding in back alleys and dim rooms, and certainly not because I lied to her. But because even in her darkest hour, she thought of protecting me.

I just hate people like that.

Chapter 5

I DIDN'T go home for two hours after Mel called the police.

When I did, Mel pretended she didn't know me. She got to the door before I opened it and told me she wasn't buying anything today and to go on now, don't bother her.

I was not in the mood for her to be funny.

I tried to push my way in. She used the Belly to keep me out. "Get that away from me," I yelled. "It's likely to blow like the *Hindenburg*." With a shocked intake of breath, Mel stood back from the doorway. I squeezed past her.

She slammed the door behind me and yelled, "You're grounded till you die and grow moldy. Don't think you can just go out the window again, because I nailed it shut."

I went to my room and saw Mel had been going through my stuff.

The whole room was tossed. She'd gone through Kerrie's stuff too. My sister was sitting on the edge of her bed, wearing her look of injured dignity. She had changed into shorts and a loose top.

I said, "You didn't get arrested."

"It was a case of mistaken identity," she said.

"I didn't mean to scare you," I said. "Not really."

"You got it all wrong," she said, flipping back to perky and brave. "It was Mel who called the police. I read them my alibi."

"Your alibi?"

"Want to see it?"

It read: "I went out right after breakfast, about 9:30 only our kitchen clock is a little fast. I rode my bike the whole time." Miss Nelda and Mr. Entwhistle had even signed for her.

"I never would have thought of an alibi."

Kerrie bobbed her head, like, *Thanks*. "It was Miss Nelda's idea."

"Remind me to go to her the next time I need a note to get out of gym."

"When I got home, Mel greeted me like I was carrying the last box of Popsicles in the whole world." All this attention had clearly made Kerrie's day; I was forgiven. "She told the policemen it was all a big misunderstanding. They said they'd let the matter drop."

I went over to open the window. I figured Mel was just talking, of course. Ranting, I mean. But she had really done it. She'd nailed my window shut. How could she do that? How was a person supposed to get any fresh air?

I said, "What's going on here?"

Kerrie said, "She's packing."

I turned around. "Where am I going?"

Mel came into the room, lugging a big suitcase. "I'm selling you to an Arab prince," she said to me.

"He isn't going to just roll me up in a carpet?"

"I'll get a better price for you with a wardrobe."

She made a threat that included the words "drive off and leave you by the side of the road" as she stuffed Kerrie's clothes into that suitcase. So I figured either she was selling Kerrie too, or I didn't have too much to worry about. Unless—

We were all going to follow Daddy to Las Vegas.

No.

That would be too pathetically desperate.

"Desperate" could be Mel's middle name, but she would never let Daddy see her pathetic. She might, on the other hand, want him to come home and find us gone. Not that she had ever done such a thing before, but she thought up revenges of this sort all the time. Usually they were revenges against me, but even then all she did was talk.

Until she nailed my window shut.

I tried thinking everything through from another angle. "You're getting back at Daddy for going off and leaving us behind. Possibly we're running off to someplace even more fun than Las Vegas."

"Something like that," Mel said.

"Disney World! Something for everyone in the family

to enjoy," I said. "And a walloping big bill for Daddy to pay off."

When she stepped across my legs to get to the bed table, she said, "Frog Slime," under her breath.

Under stress, say, in heavy traffic, Mel tends to be a name-caller. We were not driving at just this moment. Of course, we *were* both trying to occupy the narrow space between the beds. It's the only real floor space in the whole room. And the Belly appeared to have grown some in only two hours.

"You are telling Daddy we're going, right?"

"Buzzard Breath."

Lately Mel holds back on name-calling because Kerrie is a repeater. Mel doesn't want any teacher sending notes home to her about her cute little daughter's bad language. I gave her a raised-eyebrow look.

"Flea Bait." She stepped on my foot too, mostly by accident. No apology. This was clearly a stressful move we were making.

I got out a smaller version of Daddy's duffel bag and started to put some of my stuff into it, just to show how cooperative I could be. But there's only two things a person really needs on a trip: a toothbrush and money.

I only had eight dollars and change in my underwear drawer, less than five dollars in my pocket. I hunted around for my diary. All I ever kept in the diary were my savings and a wish list—the pages were otherwise blank. Except for that list of phone numbers of kids I don't really call. I'm usually working for Daddy on weekends.

Oh, and that list of books I've read, because it makes me feel smart.

I found the diary and the twenty-dollar bill I hid between the center pages. I'd been saving it for my next trip to Blue Moody's, our local music store. I decided to take the diary too, in case I needed a piece of notepaper to put in a bottle. I like to be prepared.

Kerrie followed Mel out when she left the room, but came back in only a couple of minutes. "She's writing Daddy a letter," Kerrie whispered.

That was a plain relief to me. "Go back and see what it says," I told her.

"I know what it says. We have to go see somebody's time. They left a message on the answering machine while Mel was out in the front yard, waving to the policemen."

"*Waving* to the policemen?"

"As they drove off."

"Who left the message?"

Kerrie shrugged.

Mel was sitting at the table, scribbling fast. I went straight to the machine and pushed PLAY.

"Mother's time has come. You ought to come on home right away."

That was it. No hello or good-bye. I'd never heard this woman's voice before, but it was so like Mel's it gave me goose bumps.

"Is that your sister?"

Mel didn't answer.

Chapter 6

SUNDAY STARTED out like a school morning, with a scramble to get out the door. Overnight, Kerrie forgot how to tie her sneakers. I tied them while she ate her cereal.

She asked, "It's summer, why are we in such a hurry?"

"Somebody's dying," I said. "That's what it means, that 'Mother's time has come.'"

Kerrie looked more awake immediately. "Whose mother?"

"Mel's, I guess."

"Mel's mother," Kerrie said to herself, the way she mutters over a tough math problem. Daddy's mother had died right before she was born, so grandmothers were something Kerrie knew only from storybooks.

Mel had forgotten about our appointment with the

Arab prince and acted nearly human. "Is the toast burning?" she yelled from the bathroom. "Do I smell burning toast?"

"It's rye bread," I shouted back. Our toaster always scorched the bottom edge of rye bread. I slathered peanut butter over the smoking part and ate it anyway.

"Next time, put it in upside down," Mel said, coming into the kitchen. "I need you to help me get this bag into the trunk."

Daddy's pickup is our family car. In a pinch, Mel can always call on Miss Nelda, who doesn't drive her own car but waits for a neighbor to drive it for her.

This was more than a pinch. Mel unlocked the garage and rolled out Daddy's baby blue '57 DeSoto Fireflite. Wide as two Toyotas, the Fireflite has tail fins better suited to a rocket ship than to the interstate—and, on the front, a grille like an evil grin.

The license plate reads ELVIS LVS.

We covered the seats, and we were on the road by nine o'clock, heading for Memphis. Picture three of us in the front seat, windows wide open, this whale of a car swimming among a school of Toyota guppies.

In the first twenty minutes, Kerrie moved to the backseat, then into the front seat again. This move included five stuffed animals and a heavy plastic bag filled with markers and Dover coloring books and a party favor, a flat magnetic doll with two changes of clothing.

This didn't seem to trouble Mel. Her mood was good.

Maybe too good. She sang "On the Road Again" from start to finish. Loudly. Her best singing effort is curiously flat, even though the rhythm is right. It's as if Mel can hear the music well enough but can't make her voice copy it.

She yelled, "On the road again," as a kind of chorus between other stupid songs. After about the third time, I told her to quit it. Only cuckoo clocks are set to go off every quarter hour.

Kerrie made it her business to be Kerrie, asking how far was it, would there be any kids to play with, would she get to stay up late? The usual magpie questions. She fell asleep over a coloring book around eleven-thirty. I leaned over the seat and put the cap back on her marker.

"Let me know if you get tired," I said to Mel after a while, although she only lets me drive at night. She's afraid we'll get stopped and I'll get arrested.

Actually, she's afraid that if I get caught driving, she'll be the one to get arrested. I'm a good driver. I've been driving since I was twelve. I'm five foot eight now, but Mel says I still look awful young to anyone over twenty-five.

I said, "How old do I look these days?"

She said, "Thirteen," which is of course my age. This question led her to sing about Clementine . . . shoes number nine.

Ha ha. Very funny.

The truth was, I didn't half mind the flatness of her voice when she sang songs like this. I joined her for a few rounds of "The Old Gray Mare" and "The Bear Went over the Mountain." It was fun for a little while.

But then I wondered if Daddy was having a good time where *he* was. I said, "Have you called Daddy?" and shut the whole road buddies episode down. "I mean, what if he calls? He won't know where we are till he gets home to read your note."

"I don't know where your daddy is staying," Mel said, like her voice was coming from a deep freeze frosted with ice.

"We should have a cell phone," I said.

"Brain cancer," Mel said. Kitchen appliances were not the only technologies that made her nervous.

"We ought to at least have one of those answering machines that let you call in for your messages," I said. "We could leave him a message to pick up."

Mel didn't answer right away, but took on a thoughtful look. "You know, I think we do have that kind of machine." But then she waved the idea away. "Not that it matters. I never bothered to learn how to do that."

Kerrie piped up and said, "Are we worried about Daddy?"

"Not in the least," Mel said. She gave me a sidelong look that meant I brought this up, not her. Meant *she* thought Kerrie was asleep, not listening in on something that might worry her.

Well, me too.

We made a stop for the bathroom, cheap toys, magazines,

food, and gas, in that order. Kerrie got so much loot, she didn't even ask to sit up front. It took us an hour and ten minutes to get back on the road.

We'd gotten used to air-conditioned comfort. We left the windows rolled up and turned on the air. "Just be glad this old crate has it," Mel said. "It wasn't exactly a standard item when these cars were made."

"Old crate?" I said. "Still mad at Daddy, are we?"

"*Silènzio,*" Mel said, using what is pretty much her only Italian word.

I read through a magazine article on how to do French braids. For something that looks so complex, it happens they're very easy to do.

I practiced French-braiding my hair until I thought my aching arms would fall off. "How come it's so hard to hold your arms up for, like, an hour?" I asked Mel. She didn't appear to have heard me.

"Why is the sky blue?" I asked in my whiniest voice. "Why do clouds float? Why do some caterpillars have fuzz and some don't? Why does the highway look all wet and shimmery ahead of us but when we get there it's dry? Why—"

"Shut up, Elvira."

"So why do my arms give out when I hold them up a long time?"

"All your blood runs to your feet, okay?"

"Not by me, it isn't. If biology was really adaptable, the blood would go where we need strength."

She rolled her eyes and made a little sound with her tongue.

"It's weird," I said. "Daddy is at an Elvis competition you didn't want him to go to. And we're all of a sudden headed for Graceland."

"We're not going to Graceland," Mel said. "My mother and sister live in Memphis."

"Same thing."

"Hardly. Elvira, don't look for ways to bother me. It's a long enough drive without you making it feel a whole lot longer."

I looked into the backseat and watched Kerrie breathe. Only after I was sure she was really sleeping did I lean against Mel and whisper, "Are you sure Daddy will come home?"

"Elvira, don't be ridiculous."

"Are you sure?"

"I'm very sure."

I thought this over for a minute. "Miss Lasky, my English teacher last year, said adding words like 'very' to a sentence does not make the statement stronger. It denotes an underlying weakness.'"

"Miss Lasky was a prat."

"Miss Lasky would tell me to look that up."

"I'm not Miss Lasky," Mel said. "But I do like to think I can improve your vocabulary now and again."

"Was it fun traveling with Daddy in the old days?"

"Can we avoid phrases like 'the old days'? At least until you're old enough to vote?"

"Was it fun?"

"At first," Mel said.

Mel and Daddy used to travel almost constantly. We all three did. We went from one show to another, from county fairs to seedy little bars. One Elvis party to another.

I said, "I don't remember it."

"It's all in the albums."

"Just a lot of the same pictures over and over. Daddy singing. Daddy holding me up to the camera in some motel room or over a restaurant breakfast. Daddy singing. You giving me a bath in some dingy bathtub. Da—"

"Elvira!"

"I just mean, if you hadn't written things down in the album, we wouldn't know the difference."

"Life as one long road trip is not as glamorous as it's made out to be," Mel said. "We all got tired of it. Even your daddy got tired of it. And then Kerrie was on the way."

For some reason I felt a kind of twisted satisfaction, knowing Kerrie had been a big part of the reason Mel and Daddy got off the road. Twisted because I wanted to be the reason they changed their lives. My stomach hurt.

Mel added, "Certainly the novelty of traveling with a baby had worn off."

I said, "I can hardly remember any of it. Imagine how traumatic it must have been for me, to have wiped years of my childhood from my memory."

"Look at the upside," Mel said. "It's given you a deep

well to draw from when you have a drama queen moment, like right now."

I laughed in a weak, sick way and leaned against the car door. My stomach still hurt. "What if we'd stayed on the road? What if Daddy got fat on restaurant food and used drugs to stay happy no matter how tired of it he was, like all those stories you hear?"

"Likelier I would get fat," Mel said.

Maybe. But years of sitting around waiting for his turn to get onstage would've taken their toll. He'd changed some since getting *off* the road. He'd gotten really lean and stayed tanned all the time, putting in people's fancy gardens.

He looked too good to be Elvis now, that's what Mel said when she tried to talk him out of going to Las Vegas to be judged as the best and truest Elvis.

"He looked so different," I said. "Not like when he does a party. A change came over him. He was spooky."

The truth was, I was half afraid of him the day he left, pretty much the way I would feel about anybody who looked like a dead person resurrected. I don't mean Elvis; I mean an earlier version of Daddy. In the furthest dark corners of my mind, where I was holding the doors shut, this didn't feel like a happy memory.

"Nothing inside your daddy is changed," Mel said. "These contests show off a lot of other good singers, and he has to get a mood going. It's mental."

"*He's* mental."

"It's just a costume, the hair and all."

"The hair doesn't bother me," I said. Lie.

Mel said, "Try to sleep. In case I need you to drive later."

I closed my eyes and thought about a friend whose dad bleached his ponytail, then cut it off when he got tired of it. Before that, he grew a mustache, then shaved it off; grew a beard and shaved it off too. He called this "finding himself."

My friend called this scary—every year she had to get used to a dad who looked entirely different. I never got it before, but on Friday, looking at Daddy, I knew just what she meant.

My friend's dad ended up mustacheless, beardless, and bald. "I sure hope black dye doesn't have a bad effect on hair follicles," I said.

After a moment, Mel laughed. We both laughed. Not a mean laugh—just a laugh of, well, being together. On the road again.

Because, after the first stop, Mel tried to keep the next ones under twenty minutes, we adopted a brisk walk that felt like being in fast-forward. Kerrie acted like each restroom was a tourist attraction and prowled the aisles like she was afraid of missing a good place to shop.

Once we were settled in the car again, the fast-forward feeling changed to slow motion. The highway looked the same the same the same.

After the fourth stop, we hadn't even reached Asheville.

I asked, "Do we have any cousins we don't know about?"

Mel glanced at me, then back at the road. "What does that mean?"

"Does Aunt Clare have any children?" I should point out right now that the woman's name is pronounced *Clare-ree.* Same accent on both syllables.

"Why, no, do you think I would keep that a secret?"

"You might forget to tell us, given we didn't expect to make this trip in our lifetimes."

"So far as I know, Clare is content to raise puppies." After a moment, Mel added, "Wish I'd thought of that."

I said, "Can we turn on the radio?" She'd put a ban on music to remind me I was still being punished. She even made me leave my iPod behind.

"If you want music, sing."

"When are we stopping by to see that Arab prince? I bet he'd let me listen to music."

"Don't push your luck."

Mel can be strangely lacking in the sense-of-humor department.

Like a groan, I said, "Talk radio, okay?"

Chapter 7

IT WAS getting dark when Kerrie made up her mind she couldn't take another minute in the car. Mel didn't cave, but said we ought to try for Knoxville before we stopped for the night.

I looked at the map. Knoxville would be about the halfway point, and maybe a reasonable goal for anybody who hadn't spent half their road time at rest stops.

"Climb into the backseat and keep her occupied," Mel said.

"Occupied with what?"

"Play a game. Read signs or license plates or something."

"I can do that from the front seat."

"She's your little sister," Mel said. "Just be nice to her. When you grow up, you'll be glad you did."

"How glad are you?" I asked.

"It's not the same thing at all," she said. "Climb over."

The taller I got, the harder this was to do.

"Keep your feet away from my head."

At the last place, while Mel got gas, I bought Kerrie a kind of glamour kit that looked like it might last longer than ten minutes. She hadn't taken an interest in it right away. The truth was, she was past restroom curiosity and distractions. She just wanted to know, "Are we there yet?"

Now she handed me the glamour kit. It came with glitter nail polish, roll-on body shine, fruit-flavored lip gloss, and rubbery false eyelashes. "They look like big spiders," I told her.

But I would have loved false eyelashes when I was eight years old.

Of course, I didn't get stuff like this. Mel was too afraid I would look like an Elvisette. I used to wonder why. But when I was ten, a friend of mine told her mother that Daddy was the Elvis at parties. And her mother told me how sorry she was for me.

I told her Daddy wasn't really Elvis. He wasn't dead or anything. He just pretended. I said he was good at it. She laughed like I was really stupid. After that, I knew why Mel acted so standoffish with the other mothers. I got a little standoffish with most of them too.

Using the little plastic mirror that came with the kit, Kerrie applied lip gloss to much of the area under her nose. "Try to stay in the lines," I told her.

"What lines?"

I shrugged. What did it matter?

She rolled the body shine up and down one arm experimentally. "I don't get it," she said.

I didn't get it either, but my job was to entertain the child. "Maybe you could try writing your name with it," I suggested. "On your leg."

She tried that, and it was kind of cool. If a person didn't mind having sticky stuff on their leg. Then again, she had half a tube of sticky stuff under her nose and that wasn't bothering her.

"Want me to paint your nails?"

"I want the eyelashes," Kerrie said.

I peeled the peel-off strip and pressed them into place on her eyelids. They were so heavy, she could only open her eyes halfway. "Now the nail polish," she said.

I turned on the map light to work by. I'd only finished the first hand when Mel started up. "That smell is driving me crazy."

"It won't be so bad once it dries," I said.

"I can't wait till then. Roll down the window back there. Hold your fingers outside, Kerrie."

The wind was so strong, it made wrinkles in the wet polish. But Kerrie couldn't tell. It was hard work to keep those eyelashes up; the rush of air made her shut her eyes.

I finished the other hand and promised to do her toes when we stopped for the night. She nodded, and those newly wet fingertips traded places with the others. She laid her head on the armrest to keep out of the wind.

In about ten minutes she fell asleep. I put a pillow behind her head and slid her off the armrest. I climbed back into the front seat, being careful not to bump Mel.

"Is she sleeping?" Mel asked.

"Yep."

"One more minute of that nail polish and I was gonna hurl."

You're welcome, I thought.

Mel got us a room in a motel with an indoor pool. We could all three sleep in the king-size bed—four, counting the Belly. It almost felt like we were just out here to have fun.

Mel headed for the bathroom first, still singing in that flat voice. I wanted to try to get into the pool, and they were going to shut the gate in half an hour. I dug through my duffel bag at top speed.

"I want to go to the pool too," Kerrie said. She had curled up in a huge armchair. "Would you help me take off these eyelashes?"

"Just peel them off," I said, shimmying into my suit.

"I can't."

I couldn't either. Kerrie let loose with a loud whine.

"Are you helping?" Mel said from behind the bathroom door.

"I'm trying." I flicked at the corners with a fingernail

and they wouldn't lift. I pulled very gently and Kerrie's eyelid lifted off her eyeball. That was convincing enough for me. I stopped pulling.

Mel came out of the bathroom, saying, "I think I left my toothbrush at home."

I said, "That paper strip peeled right off. The glue didn't seem all that sticky."

Mel looked at Kerrie, who peered back at her through rubber fringes. "Here, baby."

Kerrie just leaned in her direction until she rested her chin on the Belly. Mel tried to rub the lashes off with her thumb. They didn't budge.

Kerrie started to cry.

"I may just shoot you," Mel said to me.

I was not in the mood for my efforts to go unappreciated. I said, "I'm not the one who's suffering. I think you ought to shoot Kerrie."

"You have a smart mouth, Elvira Marie," Mel said. "That is not an attractive quality in a girl."

"I'll keep that in mind," I said. There might have been more of an argument, but Kerrie was now gripping Mel's maternity top and hanging from her, sobbing as if she was hanging from a cliff.

"Stand up, sweetie." Mel held down Kerrie's eyelid with her thumb and tried to peel those eyelashes off. Kerrie started to shriek. Mel stopped tugging at the eyelashes and pulled her close, in a hug.

Into Mel's ear, I said, "Maybe you have to do it like a Band-Aid, except I was scared to try it."

"Me too," Mel said. "Come on, let's go into the bathroom."

We stood Kerrie in the bathtub and held a dripping wet washcloth against her face. We tried warm water, we tried cold. We watched for the glue to change to a white color that meant it was softening up.

Kerrie sobbed the whole time.

We made her stand facing the warm water of the shower. Despite being a good swimmer, she didn't care to have water hit her in the face. She ratcheted up the sound.

I said, "Couldn't you stop crying and just talk to us?" I hated the way I sounded on the verge of hysteria myself.

When Kerrie's fingers and toes got wrinkled, we wrapped a towel around her and let her lie on the bed, a wet washcloth over her eyes. Mel said, "Does it sting, baby? Is that what's the matter?"

Kerrie didn't answer; maybe she was too worked up to hear.

Twice Mel had to get up to pee, leaving Kerrie to me. The second time she came back, I was saying to myself, over and over, *I just need ten minutes alone.*

Mel said, "Don't crash on me now." So I didn't.

The glue didn't turn white, and it didn't in any other way appear to be softening. Kerrie had altogether given up on trying to open her swollen eyes. In fact, she looked half asleep, even though Mel kept patting and jiggling and otherwise trying to comfort her. The crying was set on automatic.

"Get the other washcloth," Mel said, handing me the one that had dripped water through Kerrie's hair and into the pillow. "Of all the bright ideas I wish you'd never had—"

It was like Mel pushed a button labeled HORRIBLE GUILT, which set off another marked TEMPER. I stomped off to get the washcloth. This big-sister business was just too much work for too little gratitude.

"Jeez, somebody's gonna call the police," Mel said when I got back to her.

"You can tell them you found the missing child," I said.

Mel stood up suddenly, knocking me onto the armchair. Not that she pushed me exactly. But the force of her movement brought the Belly square into the space I was occupying. The minute I hit the bed, I yelled, "Violence! Family violence!"

"Oh, shut up," Mel muttered as she grabbed the phone and pushed 8 for the office. Over Kerrie's sobs, she said, "Can you give me directions to the nearest emergency room?"

Kerrie started to cry harder.

Mel nodded, nodded, scribbling on the edge of a menu for Chinese takeout, then slammed down the receiver and grabbed her pocketbook. "Let's go," she yelled, taking Kerrie by the hand.

Kerrie had begun to ease up by the time we reached the hospital, mainly because we got lost twice finding the place. What kind of maniac puts an emergency room at the end of no less than three curvy country roads? Well, the kind that built this hospital, that's what kind.

We went through pretty much the same scenario of pull-and-soak with one doctor and then another. Kerrie's voice was by then so hoarse, she could have been mistaken for a donkey braying, but she pushed the volume up with each doctor.

Things were not looking good. Kerrie's hair was matted to her head with tears and sweat. Her face looked like she had the kind of sunburn that wanted to peel—an overheated red with a sheer top layer of pale skin.

Mel was pretty frayed around the edges. Me too.

A third doctor was sent in, and there were actual tears standing in his eyes. I didn't know whether this meant he was real sympathetic or whether Kerrie was beyond hope. He suggested treating her with some chemical they use to remove superglue when people get their fingers stuck together.

"Are you saying they put superglue on a child's toy eyelashes?" Mel yelled. She had hit nervous overload.

"I'm saying it's what I know to do," the doctor said. Everyone had to shout to be heard over Kerrie.

"What kind of stuff is it, to melt superglue?" Mel asked.

"Basically, it's nail polish remover," the doctor said.

"You want to put nail polish remover in my baby's

eyes?" Mel came close to outreaching Kerrie for sound penetration.

"Listen, you can trust us to know what we're doing or you can take your child to another emergency room. It's only forty miles away."

"Is that any way to talk to a stricken mother?" This was Mel.

"I'm sorry, but I had a migraine when I came in here," the doctor yelled, shamefaced. "It's reaching a point now where *I* may have to be hospitalized."

Mel received this apology with uncommon good grace. She could, now and again, pull "gracious" out of a deep, linty pocket and shake it like a wrinkled handkerchief, but the finer effect wouldn't last long.

I leaned in close to Kerrie and said, "No one is going to pull on those lashes. They have some stuff that will melt the glue."

This got immediate results. She settled down to a dull roar.

One doctor used a Q-Tip to put the supermelter on. The one with a headache stood next to Mel, saying, "We don't really want her to stop crying just yet. The tears are protecting her eyes, washing the chemical away."

He'd no sooner said this than the eyelashes fell off.

Meanwhile, the hard news had sunk in for me. No one wanted to say it in so many words, but they were afraid Kerrie would end up blind.

I had this sudden picture of my sister's bike in the attic under a veil of cobwebs. Not that we actually had an attic, or I would have turned it into a bedroom a long time ago. But this didn't dim the picture of Kerrie going around with a white-tipped cane, shoulders bowed in defeat. I wanted to do a little crying myself, but the room was already at high tide.

Kerrie's eyes were so puffy, they looked like slits in a pillow. "Can you see your mother's face?" the doctor asked her.

She nodded.

"How many fingers am I holding up?"

"Two."

I let out a silent sigh of relief, one that I could see reflected in Mel's face. The doctor said, "She ought to see her pediatrician for a follow-up, but her eyesight appears to be all right."

Mel started to cry. I splashed a few tears around myself. Not that anyone noticed. The one doctor immediately told the other, headachy one that he ought to lie back down, and then they were gone, leaving the nurse to see us off.

She had instructions, like what to watch for, blurred vision and allergic reactions. I paid attention. Mel was too busy hugging Kerrie like she'd been grabbed from in front of an oncoming train. Which was pretty much the case. I felt like the whole thing was all my fault. Like I should have tested the eyelashes myself. Something.

Back at the motel, Kerrie fell onto the bed and turned on the TV. I said I would take her for a swim if they'd open the gate for us. It wasn't much, but it was all I had to offer.

She blinked her puffy eyes. "I'm too tired for swimming."

"Let's go," Mel said on her way into the bathroom for a pre-drive pee. "I can't sleep now, and I can't sit here and watch TV."

I started throwing our stuff back in the suitcases.

Kerrie worked up the indignant look that came before she set up a howl, but she really was too tired; she was having to dig deep. "Put it on hold," I said. "Remember why we're doing this? Mel's mother is dying."

Chapter 8

WE MADE Kerrie comfortable in the backseat. She fell asleep right away. But after half an hour on the road, I climbed into the backseat with her.

Mel said, "What are you doing?"

"Checking Kerrie."

"She's fine."

I climbed into the front seat. "I just felt like checking."

"It wasn't your fault," Mel said.

"I don't know what would be worse, Kerrie going blind or everybody blaming me forever. Daddy told me to keep things together."

"Listen to me, there was something wrong with that toy."

"Okay." That's what I said, but it wasn't really okay. I knew it, and probably Mel knew it.

"Kerrie's fine," Mel said. "I'm going to pull over at the next exit. You drive for a while. It will give you something different to worry about."

We switched seats every hour on the hour. Mel made me nap for twenty minutes at a time, and when I drove, she did the same. We agreed we woke up feeling like we'd been hit with a mallet, but neither of us felt sleepy when we were driving.

Sometimes we were practically the only car on the road, and other times we were surrounded by trucks. We drank coffees, but it was hard to know if they helped all that much. Mel lifted the music ban in the interest of keeping us alert.

The novelty of being on the road again had worn off, but we just kept on going. I imagined this was what Mel was like for a while before we settled down in New Hope. When all the excitement of following Daddy from town to town had worn off. Pretty much living from one parking space to another.

I didn't remember much about those years, really, just the parts that mattered to me. Getting big enough to climb on the stools in diners all by myself. Crying because the car seat was too hot. Dropping my shoes out of the car window while we were driving on the highway.

Then Mel got pregnant with Kerrie and Daddy married her. At the time, I thought the big party was for me, because I was starting kindergarten. Daddy sang, of course. "Love Me Tender," that's what he sang. The other four

Elvises sang other songs. There were plenty to choose from. Songs, I mean.

When I took over the driving at three o'clock, I said, "Mel, why did you want to go with Daddy this week if you got tired of being on the road?"

"I didn't want to go all that much," she said. "I know that must sound crazy."

"You just didn't want Daddy to go, is that it?"

"No, I—" Mel sat up straighter in the seat. "I don't want him to be sorry he missed a chance."

"That isn't what you said to him."

"I know," she said. "I just didn't want him to *want* to go."

I felt the same way, really.

I blamed the customers when Daddy first told us he was going. I could see they made him feel bad when they hired the lawn service. But when he started to want to go away, I felt like it was us he wanted to get away from. We hadn't changed, Daddy had, so then I blamed him.

Mel said, "I want him to win that contest. That's the crazy part, I guess."

"But what happens if he wins? More people ask him to sing at parties, okay, but maybe he'll have to travel more. Like we did before."

"We'll just figure it out as we go along, okay?" Mel said. "Don't worry about it right now."

"I don't know that I want him to win," I said.

"Sure you do. Not just because you love him, but because he loves you even more."

"What a parenty thing to say," I said. "Kids love their parents just as much."

"That's music to my ears, Elvira. But, just so you know, parents always love their kids more."

I got a little pain in my heart, wanting something, it felt like. But I threw her a skeptical look. "Does the Belly count?"

"Definitely," Mel said. "Practically an insurance policy. But your daddy wouldn't leave you either."

"So I'm an insurance policy too," I said. Wishing hard for it to be true. I remembered again how Daddy didn't wave good-bye, didn't look back from the end of the driveway.

But now I realized it didn't mean he was going away mad. "I think he felt bad about leaving."

Mel sat forward a little in her seat, and although I could see her only by the light on the dashboard, really, I knew the exact hopeful expression she wore on her face. She said, "Do you?"

And then, "Well, I know he did. I just forgot, I guess."

"It's like that summer when Kerrie was little and you sent me to day camp. When I came home in the afternoon, I'd be so mad that she got into my stuff, and in the morning you'd be so busy with her, changing her, warming her bottle, telling me not to add too much sugar to my cereal. I wanted to get away from you both and go see my friends."

"Elvira."

"Right up until you walked me to the bus stop," I said. "While you took me to the corner, I started to miss you so much, I wanted to stay home. I even missed Kerrie and she was right there, sucking on her pacifier while she planned how to ruin my life that day. But I missed her anyway."

"Why didn't you say?"

"I thought it was like going to the dentist, I had to. And when I got on the bus, I could've cried. Except I would've been embarrassed to be one of the crybabies, so I just sat on the side where I couldn't see you."

Mel leaned back with a sigh. "You know, that's exactly how I felt whenever we left you with a babysitter," she said. "First I thought I was desperate to get an evening out, but right before we left, I started wishing we had time for one more bedtime story, and always, for just a minute when I got in the car, I cried. Your daddy thought I was nuts."

A comfortable silence grew up between us. "Do you think everybody is as neurotic as we are?" she asked me.

I thought of things Debs's mother talked about. "Pretty much."

"There were a lot of crybabies?"

"Lots."

The funny thing, though, after I said all this to make Mel feel better, I didn't feel better. Before those customers gave Daddy a hard time, I would've said he was happy. I would've said things usually went his way. Now I wondered if he just *looked* happy.

Mel had looked happy till just lately.

When I looked over, she had fallen asleep.

Just after Daddy's momma died and we were all missing her, I started wishing for a big happy family. With Mama Rosa gone, I pictured this grandma, Mel's mother, as a sweet old lady. The kind I'd see on really old TV shows now and again.

When Mel woke up a while later, I said, "I always wondered about this grandmother."

"Your daddy and I hardly talk about her, Elvira," Mel said, sounding cranky. "I'm amazed the whole thing didn't just go over your head."

"Other kids visit their grandparents, they get birthday presents from them. If we didn't do Santa Claus, do you think I wouldn't notice that either?"

"Good point."

"I wondered if she was the kind of grandmother who baked pies and stuff."

Mel laughed a little. "That's not the test of the perfect grandmother."

"No, but it's a good start." I didn't say it, but I used to bury my face in my pillow at night and wish for that grandmother. Speeding down the highway, I made a little wish that my wish was about to come true.

It was four in the morning the last time I gave the wheel up to Mel. After that, I fell into a deep black sleep. When Mel woke me, I followed her out of the car without a question. I thought I was dreaming. Halfway across the yard, I realized we'd arrived.

Chapter 9

THERE WERE two floors and a big porch that wrapped around, making a curved corner. A small round upstairs room was topped off with a roof like a pointy cap. The house was cute. Pretty, even, with periwinkle blue shutters and those fish-scale shingles around the roofline. Daddy would have admired the flower beds.

We shivered as we climbed the steps. It was summer, but we hadn't had any sleep to speak of, and it was early and damp. We were cold. After the third time Mel rang the doorbell, we tried peering in the windows, but the blinds were pulled tight.

She looked at me and said, "Maybe there's nobody here. Maybe they've taken her off to the hospital." Another shiver made her teeth chatter.

"Wouldn't your sister have told you that?"

"I don't know," Mel said. She rang the bell again.

I tried out the porch swing. This was, after all, my grandmother's house. "Shh," Mel said when the chains creaked. I got right up again, but certain things still interested me. I'd never thought of Mel's mother as someone with a porch swing.

I said, "Maybe you should call Clare."

"*Aunt* Clare."

"*Aunt* Clare, then," I said. "It's cold out here."

Mel said, "I'd just drive on over to the hospital, but it's been so many years, I have no idea where to go."

I looked at my watch. "It's only ten minutes to six. Maybe she doesn't get up at the crack of dawn."

Mel rang the doorbell, rang it like the bell between classes. No one could be sleeping through that. As if to prove my point, the upstairs lights went on in a house down the street.

Kerrie's head appeared in the backseat window of our car. We had about sixty seconds before she started yammering about a restroom. She'd slept through our last two stops.

There was a sound from inside the house, a kind of thump. I gave Mel a triumphant look, but Mel said, "Maybe she's in there and needs help." She rang the bell again.

"If she can't open the door, ringing that bell won't help."

"You're right. You stay here and I'll go around and look in the kitchen window."

"No, let me," I said. The Belly had grown huge in only

the three days since Daddy left; it was like some horrible science fiction movie come true. "You might slip on the wet grass."

Right then, the front door opened. Mel and I both jumped a little. There hadn't been any footsteps. No old-lady voice calling, *Whoooo is it?*

"Momma," Mel said, like she was the one woken up.

The grandmother was tall, like Mel and me, dressed in a short-sleeved cotton bathrobe. Her silver hair had been wrapped in toilet tissue that had loosened in her sleep and now hung in loops around her head. The woman looked like she had never opened the door on such an unwelcome sight as Mel and me.

I reminded myself this was just Mel's mother and she didn't look like a morning person. Mel isn't a morning person either. We'd driven through the night, was all.

In a flat, tired voice, the grandmother said, "He's left you."

Mel put her hands protectively over the Belly. She said, "As a matter of fact, Momma, the girls and I came to see how you are."

The car door slammed shut and the grandmother glanced past us. "I'd ask you to park that behind the bushes," she said, like the car was part of a scary movie she was watching, "but I don't have enough bushes in one spot to hide it."

Mel said, "Then it's in as good a place as any."

The grandmother was pretty rude, even for six in the morning. We weren't looking our best, I knew that, but then neither was she.

Kerrie came up on the porch, carrying her sack of toys like she had every confidence we were staying. One look at the grandmother's face and she slipped her hand into mine. I shook Kerrie off, but not in a mean way. I wanted us to look strong, to be strong. I hoped she got that.

Each year, the grandmother gifted Kerrie and me with a Life Savers Christmas box of different-flavored rolls of candy. By mail. Only the return address showed where it came from. Daddy would always say to Mel, "We can just drive over there," like she lived only a few blocks away.

Mel always said, "Over my dead body."

I knew the history on this, but Mel and Daddy were married now. How long could Mel's mother stay mad that they didn't get married sooner? And how long could Mel stay mad that her mother got mad?

Daddy would try again. "One sight of the girls would soften her right up."

"Don't bet on it." Then Mel would send this woman a Christmas card, tucking my picture and Kerrie's into it. It was not something I ever brought up, but if someone had shoved a microphone in my face and said, "Who do you think is to blame?" I'd have guessed it was Mel who was still mad and cheating Kerrie and me out of a quality grandmother experience.

Until now.

Kerrie piped up then in her little voice meant to remind people she's a child. Because Kerrie is, unlike Mel and myself, petite, people put up with it. "Could I use your bath-room? I really need to tinkle."

Because she's cute, some people even encourage it.

"Do you mean you need to pee?" the grandmother asked.

Well, hoo-ray.

Kerrie nodded meekly.

The grandmother stepped back and motioned with one hand. "Go all the way down the hall and through the kitchen. There you will find the johnny house."

Kerrie looked her in the eye and said, "Does that mean it's outside?"

The grandmother lowered her voice an octave to say, "Definitely not."

Kerrie walked right inside, like one of those kamikaze pilots she watched on the History Channel. She didn't cower in the least.

The grandmother waited until Kerrie had disappeared from sight before asking, "Is there something wrong with that child?"

Mel said, "Why do you ask?"

"She's short."

Mel said, "She's a child."

"She knows it only too well."

"Just be nice to her," Mel said. "She'll quit it a whole lot sooner."

The grandmother's eyes grew round. "Be nice to her?"

A point for Mel, who added, "You're a little daunting at six in the morning, Momma."

"That's the nicest thing you've said to me in years." Witty, the grandmother.

Most kids wouldn't want this woman for a grandmother. I wasn't sure I wanted her. But something about her struck me as, well, interesting.

"It's what kids do when there's another baby on the way, that's all," Mel said. "She's pretty sure babies must be irresistible."

"Not to me," the grandmother said.

"Probably she'll figure that out. Are you going to let us stand here and catch our death, or do we all have to tell you we want to tinkle?"

She gave Mel one more look I couldn't read and said, "You might as well come in. I was just going to have breakfast. In an hour or so."

"We can go away and come back later," I said, not stepping forward. I admit it, I wanted to wring an actual welcome out of her.

"I'm not sure my heart could take it," she said, holding the door open wider.

There was something in her eyes when she looked at me. Curiosity. Something. She looked away before I could quite know what it was.

Mel stepped around me. "We should have called first," she said, which was only the simple truth. The woman would've had a chance to get that mess off her head.

Chapter 10

I FOLLOWED Mel inside. The hallway had a faint smell. I thought of Miss Nelda, who was a little too enthusiastic about those plug-in air fresheners. But she always worried that her house would get what she called "that old-lady smell." I wondered if this was it.

"To tell you the truth," Mel said, "I was under the impression there was some kind of emergency."

"Oh, well, the fire is out," the grandmother said.

"What fire?" Mel asked. She went from Mel the Invader to Smokey the Bear in a heartbeat.

"The one in the warshing pantry," the grandmother said.

"We're talking about a real fire?" Mel asked, her voice rising. "As in flames and smoke?"

"The very same."

Smoke. That's what I smelled. I was really glad it wasn't the old-lady smell. They were more or less moving toward the kitchen, the grandmother shuffling along in big fluffy slippers, tissue paper afloat around her ears. I had time to look into doorways.

"When did this happen?" Mel asked.

"More'n a week now," the grandmother said.

"Did you have smoke inhalation? Is that why you were in the hospital?"

"I didn't go to the hospital," the grandmother said irritably.

The hospital idea had come to Mel while she was standing on the porch or maybe while she was driving through the night. She said, "Right, right. But you said there was a fire, Momma."

"I just wanted to press the wrinkles out of a dress. I was in a hurry to go and I forgot to turn off the iron," the grandmother said. "I wasn't even in the house when it started. I missed the whole thing."

The place was bigger than I'd thought at first. Big central hallway. Two dark sitting rooms at the front, a dining room midway, and on the other side, what looked like the grandmother's bedroom. The lamp next to her bed gave me a good view of this room. A wall of bookshelves. Dark woods. Everything else faded and tired-looking, even the book covers.

"No one was hurt?" Mel was asking.

"My neighbor saw the smoke and ran over here to douse the fire. His eyebrows were singed right off. He looked a bit overbaked for a few days, and now he's peeling. But other than that, no."

"Well, that's good," Mel said. I knew she was wondering the same thing I was: What did her sister's message mean?

"If I'd had to count on the fire department, I'd probably be standing on *your* doorstep this morning."

Mel looked stricken, and the grandmother laughed.

It *was* kind of funny.

The kitchen was just the kind Mel was always yearning for. Old-fashioned, mainly. There was a plain white gas stove. And a pretty, green woodburner held a collection of old bowls on the stovetop.

But even that stove wasn't enough to distract the eye from the window over the sink. It was brand-new, with the store label in one corner. The wall above and the cabinets around had a dark color over the paint job, like storm clouds.

"I thought you said the fire was in the laundry room," Mel said.

"This is an old fire," the grandmother said. "I left the little window fan running while I went to the store. I'd done that a hundred times, but this time it overheated, burst into flame, and ate the curtains."

"It must have eaten the window too," Mel said, in that tone she uses when she thinks she's about to catch me in a lie.

"That window always stuck going up and down," the grandmother said. "I figured I'd just as soon start off with a new one that slides easy."

"So you had two fires."

"There's nothing to show for this one but scorch marks," she said, as if this ought to close the subject.

Kerrie came into the room from the other side, and joined us as we sat down at the enamel-topped table in the middle of the kitchen. There was another table at the side, in a kind of breakfast nook that looked more appealing, but I gathered it hadn't yet been decided if we were going to stay. Summit meetings were likely held at this table.

"So how many fires have you had?" Mel said, sounding too casual, the way she does when the lie-catching voice isn't getting her anywhere.

"I'm not in the business, you know," the grandmother said. "The arson business. Unless you count burning down the shed."

"Let's count that," Mel said, "if it burned down. It burned to the ground?"

"Accidents happen," the grandmother said, her eyes narrowing.

"Yes, they do," I said, hoping to avoid a fight.

Mel said, "How long ago was the window?"

"It's been a couple of months now."

"And the iron was about two weeks ago?"

"Not quite."

"One of those comes-in-threes things," I said. "Like

when you break a glass, it always happens again real soon, and then again."

They went quiet. So I went quiet.

We all sat like we were there for a game but somebody forgot the cards. Neither Mel nor the grandmother would meet anyone's eyes. Kerrie and I waited to see if we were playing Hearts or War.

Mel said, "Could I make us some coffee, Momma?"

"Lands, yes," the grandmother said, coming to life. "You children haven't eaten yet, have you?"

Kerrie and I shook our heads. We hadn't eaten.

"Start the coffee, Melisande," she said, getting up. "Give me seven minutes to make myself look human and we'll make some breakfast." She hurried out of the kitchen, pulling at the loops of paper and balling them up in her hands.

Seven minutes seemed an odd number. I looked at the clock, saying, "Can I do anything?"

"Sit still," Mel said. She found coffee in one cabinet, mugs in another; both times exactly where she expected them to be. "And don't try to mediate."

I said, "Mediate?"

"Be quiet. You don't have to help me deal with her."

I watched the clock and sure enough, in seven minutes the grandmother was back, looking like a new woman. A new *old* woman, okay, but she looked pretty good, like she could be in a commercial for a breakfast cereal or something.

Mel and the grandmother moved around the kitchen like it was only yesterday they'd cooked breakfast together.

"I expected to find Clare here," Mel said as the grandmother passed her eggs and butter from the refrigerator.

"Your sister has her own home," the grandmother said. I thought her tone suggested Aunt Clare ought to stay in it. Then again, the grandmother put that tone in most of what she said.

"Me too," Mel said. "But I'm here."

"Why?" The grandmother sounded like it was the last thing she'd ever expect, that Mel would be there.

Mel said, "I thought you needed me."

"You had a clairvoyant experience?"

"You have not mellowed with age, Momma."

The grandmother said cheerfully, "Now that's a pure fallacy, mellowing with age. People become more and more comfortable with who they are as they get older, not less and less. For some, that may appear to be a mellowing. In my case, it isn't."

Mel sighed loudly.

It occurred to me that the grandmother wasn't unfriendly so much as it was that she enjoyed an air of debate to her conversation. Seen from the back, she was a dance of elbows to the beat of eggs cracked against an iron frying pan.

I glanced at Kerrie at the exact moment she looked in my direction. She raised her eyebrows, quirked her mouth down at one corner. I had never felt so close to her before.

Chapter 11

"SO YOU had this clairvoyant experience and you just upped and hauled your children over here, lickety-split."

Mel dug into her pocket for the car keys and tossed them to me. "Pull it up closer to the house," she said.

The grandmother arched an eyebrow. "She drives?"

"It's the driveway, Momma, not the interstate." Kerrie took on an alert expression, hearing Mel come so close to telling her mother a lie. She didn't say a word.

"That car must take a lot of gas," the grandmother said.

"We hardly ever use it," Mel said. "It's more of an investment."

"Risky," the grandmother said. "Investing in a business you could lose over a fender bender."

"You can replace a window, Momma, and I can replace

a fender." Mel looked at me. "Elvira, would you move that car?"

I hated to go, but I figured Kerrie wouldn't miss much and would be happy to tell me anything worth knowing. It wasn't only that I worried I'd miss something, I felt a little left out, the way the grandmother talked like I wasn't really there. She hardly looked at me.

I moved the car, even though there was this old fellow—Daddy says don't say "old man," it sounds mean—standing across the street, watching me do it. He had a white paper sack in one hand, and when I got out of the car, he waved to me and started to come over.

Uh-oh, I thought, because he looked a little strange. At first I thought it was because he wore the standard golf pro outfit—yellow plaid pants, sparkling white shirt, sunburn. Then I saw the only really strange thing about him was his eyebrows; they were unusually sparse and crinkled, so his face looked strangely bare. But he had a friendly twinkle in his eyes, even if it was just a reflection from his shirt.

He said, "Are you offering a car-parking service in the neighborhood?"

"I'm visiting my grandmother," I said.

"I have this package for her, if you wouldn't mind delivering it." He offered me the paper sack.

I took it.

We told each other thank you a little awkwardly, and I went back inside.

I didn't knock. Going down the hall as quietly as possible, I heard the grandmother say, "He's still in that land-scaping business?"

"He's doing very well, and you'd know it, Momma, if you bothered to read my letters."

I didn't know Mel wrote to her mother.

It got me thinking. If Daddy offered to drive Mel to see her mother now and again, he thought it was important. If Mel wrote letters, she must've hoped the grandmother would write back.

"He ought to have come with you," the grandmother was saying. "It's a hard trip for a woman in your condition to make."

The grandmother had put Mel on the spot, but Kerrie said, "We stopped at a motel with a pool."

"Oh, you don't let them get into a heated pool?" the grandmother said, letting the subject of what Daddy ought to do slide. "Those are just swarming with bacteria. They could pick up I don't know what!"

Mel smiled as I slid onto the chair. "Beats me, Momma, if you didn't sound like an old grandmomma right then."

The grandmother ignored her. "You girls want your scrambled eggs on the toast or next to it?"

"Next to it, please," Kerrie said. She had pulled the coloring books out and spread her markers in front of her.

"This paper sack, and whatever's in it, is for you," I said. The grandmother looked over her shoulder, a tad flustered for a moment, but then said, "Sesame-seed bagels. We can eat them instead of toast, if you like them."

"Bagels, Momma? After all those years of insisting we eat whole wheat bread?"

"It's good for you," the grandmother said. "That doesn't mean I can't eat anything else."

"True," Mel said. "Where do you get these?"

"A neighbor has them mailed in from New York," the grandmother said. "He has relatives up there."

Mel glanced at me. "Is he cute?"

The grandmother looked around, so I shrugged. But when she turned back, I nodded. Cute. Mel grinned.

Mel's momma didn't sit. She kept a plate on the counter and took bites from her toasted bagel as she went about the kitchen, watering her single houseplant and setting out food for a cat I hadn't yet seen.

At the same time, she covered the usual territory—what grades were we in now and did we play any musical instruments, like that. I reported I played the guitar. Kerrie said she took ballet and then took a bite of her scrambled eggs. She started coloring as she chewed.

She didn't say she'd taken ballet happily for one week. Or that for ten months and three weeks since, it had taken bullying and bribery to get her to the two classes a week Mel was paying for. Kerrie liked tutus and tiaras. The hard work of ballet class didn't appeal to her in the least.

"Ballet is important for girls," the grandmother said. "It makes them graceful, but it also makes them strong."

Kerrie didn't mention she was looking forward to month twelve, when the contract Mel signed would expire.

That we were all looking forward to that. Without even looking at each other, neither Mel nor I blew Kerrie's cover story.

As we ate our breakfast, the sounds in the room were the clink of our forks on the plates, the squeaky progress of Kerrie's markers, and the grandmother doing a little kitchen cleanup.

The grandmother finally sat down, asking, "This one that's coming, do you know whether it's a boy or a girl?"

"No, I didn't want the doctor to tell me."

"So you weren't trying for a boy?"

"If you must know, Momma, we weren't trying." Mel pushed her chair back from the table so she could stretch her legs.

From outside, a voice very like Mel's, should she have been imitating an ambulance siren, called, "Yoooo-hoo, Momma." We had no more than put down our forks when a woman came in through the back door.

The grandmother's voice was quick and sharp. "What on earth is the matter with you, Clare, squealing at me like that? The neighbors will think the house is afire again."

"Why, Momma, there's a strange car in the driveway—" Aunt Clare stopped, open-mouthed, and put her hand to her chest.

"It's an investment," the grandmother said, and she was too quick for me, I couldn't tell whether it was sarcasm. Besides, Aunt Clare was something of a distraction. Her voice on the machine was so like my mother's that I'd expected some version of Mel. Tall and flat-chested mostly, nothing showy about her.

But Aunt Clare was so blond, so rounded where Mel had never been, so . . . glittery, with earrings and beads on her shirt. Her shorts were styled to look like a little skirt. It was barely eight o'clock in the morning and already she was dressed like Memphis Barbie.

"Well, if it isn't Melisande," she said. "Isn't this a bolt from the blue."

"Is it?" Mel asked in a cool voice.

"You haven't changed one bit," Aunt Clare said. "Or is that one of those joke pillows you've stuffed up under there?"

My breath caught.

Mel said, "No joke." Which is not to say that Mel took this crack about the Belly all that well. I saw that she wanted to look like a woman who had never heard of raging hormones. She might even want to trade places with a woman who wore beads before the first soap opera of the day came on the TV.

Mainly, I saw how Aunt Clare wanted to hurt Mel and she had; Mel looked like she could be poured under a door. I hated Mel's little sister at that moment.

"Melisande always had the awfullest sense of humor," Aunt Clare said, looking at me. "You must be Elvira."

"Want to try these false eyelashes?" I reached for Kerrie's sack. "They've only been used once, and they're just the thing for that touch of glamour."

Aunt Clare gave me a suspicious look. "I don't believe I'd be interested."

"Too bad," I said, and began to spread jelly on my last bit of toast.

"Pretty girls," Aunt Clare said, eyeing Kerrie, who did not look flattered. Kerrie had picked up on the general air of a fight might break out. But a little color came back to Mel's face.

"Is there any coffee left?" Aunt Clare asked after a long, awkward moment during which only the scraping of my knife could be heard. "Aren't you going to offer me some, Momma? Ask me to sit down?"

"Pour yourself some coffee and sit," the grandmother said.

Aunt Clare used exaggeratedly polite tones to say, "Why don't you roll out the red carpet, Momma?"

The grandmother was not embarrassed. "Don't wait for engraved invitations, the mailman's bag is already heavy enough."

"If you aren't just the limit," Aunt Clare said, doing exactly as she was told, pulling an extra chair from beside the refrigerator. "Just because I'm family is no reason to let your manners slack off."

"Then I guess I ought to tell you that's my chair I stood on to wash some of the soot off the cabinets. Put a dish towel over it if you don't want to dusty your shorts."

"You shouldn't be standing on chairs at your age, Momma," Aunt Clare said.

"I don't have a right way to get up there," the grandmother said. I could see the grandmother had tried. There were rounded shapes at the bottom of the stains to show where she had wiped them away until she couldn't reach anymore. She added, "I need a step stool."

"I took the step stool, Momma, so you *wouldn't* get up there. The last thing I need is for you to fall off of it."

"Step stools are for stepping on," Kerrie said. "I learned that in Health and Safety."

"Been here long?" Aunt Clare asked Mel, like she was the other person waiting at a bus stop. "Tony with you?"

"He had to be away for a few days," Mel said. This was her chance to tell them more, but she didn't, pretty much leaving the impression his trip was business as usual.

"Mel came to see how I was doing," the grandmother said. "She seemed to think I might be in the hospital. What do you make of that?"

Mel said, "I don't know where I got that idea."

Kerrie looked up from her coloring book, saying, "On the way here—"

"We passed a big hospital," Mel said.

"But we didn't stop by," I added, and Kerrie remembered to take another bite of her egg. She went back to coloring.

"You said you thought I was in the hospital," the grandmother said, showing some nettle.

I said, "She asked about the hospital after you told her you'd had a fire."

"I remember," the grandmother said. "I remember things fine."

"Fine," Aunt Clare said, like a weak echo.

The grandmother fixed Mel in her sights. "I have this idea Clare called you and told you to come on out here."

"I felt like you ought to get to know my girls, Momma," Mel said, her eyes shining into the grandmother's. I didn't think she ought to lie for her sister. I didn't think Aunt Clare deserved it.

"Isn't this a wish come true, Momma?" Aunt Clare asked, concentrating on adding some more sugar to her coffee. Rule number one for telling a lie: She should meet the grandmother's eyes, the way Mel did.

Chapter 12

"I CAN get up there without a stool," I said, pointing to the smoky walls.

The grandmother looked interested. "Can you?"

"She no doubt can," Mel said. "She used to get up on the counters to look in the cabinets for cookies. She made me think of a pigeon on a ledge."

Aunt Clare met the grandmother's glance, and it was apparently decided to ignore Mel's offering of this piece of my personal history. I knocked off my shoes, put the chair in front of the sink, and climbed up. This brought everybody out of their chairs to look up, like one of those scenes where everyone points up at Superman.

With a slight stretch, I could put the flat of my palm to the ceiling. I could clean it. I would clean it, even though we'd received only the most grudging welcome. Grudging welcomes did seem to be the grandmother's style.

"I could get up there too," Kerrie said, only because she wanted to be included. She was never a climber.

"You still won't be tall enough to reach," Mel said to her. "And if I catch you trying, I will snatch you bald-headed."

"Melisande!" The grandmother put her hands over Kerrie's ears. "Is that any way to speak to a child?" My sister looked a little bewildered. Mel tended to make colorful threats, but we never took her seriously.

"It's the way you always talked to me, Momma," Mel said, dabbing soap onto a sponge she found in the sink. She handed it to me.

"This sponge is going to get all black," I said after the first swipe.

"Don't bother about it," Mel said. "It'll wash or it'll throw. We can get more."

"You can get them right there under the sink," the grandmother said helpfully. She started messing with spray bottles and drying rags and offers of iced tea. All things the job didn't need, but I liked the feel of this shared activity. We talked very little, we fought not at all.

Kerrie, meanwhile, showed Aunt Clare her body roll-on, and the both of them wrote their names on their legs. Kerrie told her sad story of the eyelashes. I glanced at Mel and she gave me a firm look, one that said, *Who cares if she tells?*

There was some tsk-tsking and a remark from the grandmother that we were all lucky Kerrie didn't go blind. I didn't look down to see if any of it was aimed at me. Wall washing, that was all the meaning in my life.

The water dripped down my arm and off the sharp point of my elbow, and Mel dried the counter before it became slippery. Every couple of minutes, I handed a blackened sponge down to Mel for rinsing and resoaping, until it wouldn't come clean anymore.

The smoke stains were oily, and there had been an old coat of kitchen grease on the cabinets before the fire. I was tired, but I was also glad I had something to do.

"I wish I could offer to help with the cabinets," Clare said three times in about an hour. "If I had known we'd be working on a kitchen project, I would have dressed accordingly."

"We have enough hands at work here," Mel said.

Mel was no doubt happy to have Kerrie occupied, even if the eyelash fiasco was now known to all. Although it did seem to me it ought to be Mel sitting in the chair and Aunt Clare soaping the sponge. No one said anything along these lines, but Aunt Clare couldn't leave it alone.

After a few harmless remarks about the trip we made, she began to take potshots at Mel again. "How are you feeling?" Aunt Clare asked. "Do you find pregnancy more of a drain, being an older mother and all?"

"Not in the least," Mel said, a hard edge creeping into her voice. "It makes me feel twenty years old all over again."

"Well, you look wonderful," Aunt Clare said in a falsely flattering tone.

In fact, Mel looked like someone who had driven through the night without sleeping more than a few minutes at a time, and there was no one there who didn't know it. I looked at Mel with what she sometimes called "a speaking glance," but she only shook her head as if to say, *Don't get into it with her.*

So all right, I wouldn't. But I couldn't keep entirely quiet either.

"Why is it that the *e* in Clare is pronounced but the final *e* in Melisande is silent?" I asked, in the direction of the ceiling.

It seemed they were stumped for an answer.

I handed Mel the sponge and saw that she'd thinned her lips till they were practically gone. I grinned and she laughed.

That made me laugh in this strange contorted way, like my voice came through a spiral straw. The grandmother and Clare didn't see anything funny. Mel laughed harder, like she was crying, and then I did too. Laughed so hard, I felt weak in the belly.

"They're both punch-drunk," the grandmother said.

Kerrie said, "What does that mean?"

Mel slapped my leg with the sponge before she gave it back to me; our laughter had become long, wheezy moans.

"They're Cracker Jacks," Aunt Clare said. "Nutty popcorn."

"Because they're tired," the grandmother said. "Both of you come sit down."

"No, no," Mel said, and sputtered into the crook of her elbow. "We're fine. Really. Give us a minute."

Kerrie opened the nail polish, ready to do Aunt Clare's manicure.

This made it possible for Mel to shift gears. "Take that stuff outside. It turns my stomach over."

"Well, we surely don't want to do that," Aunt Clare said as she picked up the nail polish. "Let's go out on the veranda, Kerrie, the way ladies do."

Just the movement in the room seemed to help me get back to work. I had a little more energy; just enough to finish, I figured. After a time, Aunt Clare called into the kitchen to say that she and Kerrie were going for a walk.

"The way ladies do," the grandmother said.

Chapter 13

"COME ON down," Mel told me once. "You've been up there for nearly three hours."

"I'm not done yet."

"Trade places with me," the grandmother said to Mel. She was the one, then, to hand me the sponge and wipe the counter dry. Mel sat down on the floor, cross-legged, to go on cleaning the lower cabinets.

After a time, Mel said, "It's getting too hot for this, you're dripping sweat on me."

"I'm nearly done. Let me finish." I was tired to the point of feeling dizzy, but I didn't want to quit just yet. "I might find out where the cookies are hid."

The grandmother laughed. "You let me know about it

if you find any. But don't worry, we'll buy some before the day is out."

I grinned down at her, but right away her eyes slid away, almost as if she was afraid of me. That couldn't be true. When I had my diary to hand, I'd start a new list: Things to Figure Out About the Grandmother.

In the end, we were lucky the counter crossed the entire wall so we could go from corner to corner without leaving a visible line between clean and still dirty. The kitchen looked brighter, or at least it looked cleaner, which was a lot to say.

There were some oddly stubborn stains left on the wall that looked like drifting smoke. "Nothing a coat of paint won't cure," the grandmother said. "Time to eat something."

We fried bologna and layered it with lettuce and tomato in sandwiches. We'd just sat down when I noticed the cat's dish. The food hadn't been touched.

"I haven't seen your cat."

The grandmother looked at the dish. "My lands. You two start, I'll be right back." She picked up the dish and headed out of the kitchen, and maybe upstairs. "Go ahead, start without me."

We wouldn't, of course. Mel touched her finger to a flap of bologna and tasted it, gave me the thumbs-up sign. I grinned, but we both turned at the sound of Kerrie pounding up the back steps at full speed.

She came in, pink with happy excitement. "You'll never guess what Aunt Clare has at her house."

"Puppies," I said, the way somebody might say "roaches."

"You knew?" Kerrie asked. "How did you know?"

"I guessed."

"I brought you girls something," Aunt Clare said, coming into the kitchen with a golden bundle of fluff in her arms. "Mel, are you going to shoot me if I give these girls a dog?"

"Probably," Mel said.

"You don't just give people's children a dog without asking first," I said, standing up. I wasn't going anywhere; I just couldn't stay in the chair.

"I thought you'd love a puppy," Aunt Clare said, for once nearly at a loss for words. She had her hands full of wriggling puppy. It looked like its every gene was screaming, *New place to mess up. Let's get going.*

"Elvira," Mel said, "I'll be the mother."

"It isn't right," I said. "First she makes a crack about you having another baby, and then she waltzes in—"

"What does that mean, a crack?" Aunt Clare said as the grandmother's footsteps could be heard coming downstairs. "What am I being accused of?"

"That crack," I said, "about Mel being an *older* mother? That was entirely uncalled-for. Waltzes in here," I continued, "like Santy Claus with long glittery nails, and expects us to take on a puppy that's gonna need to be house-trained."

"If you don't want this puppy," Aunt Clare said, getting mad, "you don't have to take it."

"Oh, no," Kerrie cried. She threw herself on the floor for a big sobfest. The puppy went still, its brown eyes fixed on me, tongue lolling.

"Land's sake, what's going on in here?" the grandmother wanted to know as she sailed in. Unless she was deaf as a post, she had heard every word on her way into the room.

"This child has the manners of a goat," Aunt Clare said, pointing at me. Kerrie pounded on the floor with her fist and gave us what was very likely her version of the same opinion, but we couldn't understand a word she said.

"My children and their manners," Mel said, "have not been your concern from the day they were born. One day's acquaintance does not make you qualified to comment."

From the floor, Kerrie wailed, "Bu-wha-gih-ih-ih-anh-doh-kik."

Mel said, "Kerrie, get up off the floor. Go back outside. I don't want to listen to this."

Kerrie did.

Maybe it was just the novelty of having two fairly new family members for an audience. Or maybe she looked over and saw the grandmother had turned a glinty eye on her. Raspy sobs echoing through the hallway as she headed for the front porch, she went.

"That doesn't even look like it'll be a *small* dog," I pointed out. "We don't have enough room for it."

"Why's that? Where are you living?" Aunt Clare said,

which made for a silence in the room. Somehow I'd managed to open us up to some further insult.

"Just take the dog home for now, Clare," Mel said. "I need to talk to my girls."

"I didn't mean to cause trouble," Aunt Clare said. "Really, I didn't."

"I know it." This was Mel. I had my doubts.

Looking straight at Mel, I said, "I'm not changing diapers, and I'm not picking up wee-wee pads either."

"Take that dog outside, Clare," the grandmother said. "Put it in the boot box and leave the top open. Did you and Kerrie eat?"

"No, we got involved with the puppies," Aunt Clare answered, never making a move for the door. But this answer got Mel to her feet.

The grandmother said, "A lot of this could have been avoided if you had simply fed that child. She hasn't had nothing but a plate of eggs since I laid eyes on her. None of us have."

I said, "Kerrie can have my sandwich."

"How could you never get around to eating?" Mel asked Aunt Clare in an annoyed tone. She began to take the sandwich makings back out of the fridge. "Don't I remember you bragging about how your husband always came home for lunch? Didn't you feed him?"

Aunt Clare and the grandmother looked a look at each other, which I thought must mean they took this remark as a crack of Mel's own. It might have been. But Mel glanced up and caught that look. "Clare? What is it?"

"My husband left me, Melisande. Nearly eight months ago."

I waited to see how we were to take this. "Oh, Clare," Mel said with real sympathy. "How awful. You know I didn't know. Why didn't you write or something? Surely that's as serious as—"

"As Momma losing her marbles?" the grandmother said. "I hope I am more a matter for discussion than Clare's husband flying the coop. I am family."

"So was he, Momma," Aunt Clare said, "until he—you make me sound like a cage."

"Sorry, Clare," the grandmother said. "That was unintended."

"I didn't know what to say to you, Mel," Aunt Clare said, sinking into a chair at the table, holding the puppy. It had begun to chew on the collar of her blouse. "I still don't. After all the hair Momma and Daddy raised over you running off with Tony Ruggiero, and you have these lovely girls. And I didn't stand up for you. I know you wished I would."

"Why didn't you, then?" Mel said. "I know you liked him. You kept saying how cute he was, right up till I packed a bag to go with him."

"Well, that's just it," Aunt Clare said. "I didn't think you'd run off with him. If I had been a less popular girl, it would have destroyed me socially—"

"Stop right there," Mel said, frosting over. "I know where you're going with this. But you aren't a cheerleader or class secretary anymore, Clare, and I do have these lovely girls. Tony's girls."

I was proud of Mel. It made me crazy sometimes when she could be so quick to decide what she thought and I found myself in the wrong, the way Aunt Clare was suddenly finding herself, but for the moment I was proud of the way Mel stood up for herself.

"Well, I can't feel right about it now, Melisande. Not after my very perfect marriage falls apart and he leaves me with a bunch of dogs to take care of."

I had to admit this was an unexpected side to Aunt Clare. Genuine.

Mel had begun to fry more bologna. She said, "Elvira, will you take that dog outside for Aunt Clare? Send Kerrie back in here."

Chapter 14

I SHOT a look at Mel. How old did I have to get before she wouldn't keep sending me out of the room just as things got interesting? I took the dog, trying hard not to notice the softness of golden puppy fur. Or the puppy's wriggly warmth.

I would give Mel three minutes and not a second more.

The screen door slapped shut behind me. "Inside," I said to Kerrie, who was on the back steps.

She was already getting up. "Can I hold her?"

"Not till you eat," I said. "Those orders come from higher up."

She let her fingers trail over the puppy as she passed me. We'd missed having a dog. I just didn't want this one. Not much, anyway. Even though it licked my hand.

It would grow to be more than twice Hound's size, was my guess.

I opened the boot box on the back porch and took out the one pair of rubber boots it contained. It was a long box, the puppy could run back and forth until it got tired enough to sleep.

It started to whine the minute I put it down. It tried to climb the sides, and when that didn't work, it sat back to study the situation.

I wondered if it was really the dog that bothered me so much. If I was honest with myself, I'd had a mood coming on right before Kerrie came into the kitchen with the news about the dog. I was tired, real tired, and still hungry.

I decided it didn't matter. Cleaning up after a puppy wasn't going to improve my mood one bit.

The puppy begged me for help.

I wanted to be able to drop a towel in there, something soft for it, but I had nothing to offer. The whine became a kind of yodel and I ducked back into the house, hoping the puppy would just quiet down.

Mel stood at the stove, where she was still frying bologna. Kerrie had been given my sandwich. It was pretty much a case of she and Aunt Clare had shown up in time to put their napkins in their laps. There was something of a family resemblance here.

Aunt Clare said, "We thought you'd end up some kind of gypsy"—at this Mel made a delicate snorting sound—

"following his polished black hair and tight pants from one honky-tonk to another."

"You'd have known better if you'd given him half a chance, Clare," Mel said.

"I'm only saying that's how it *looked,* sugar. Plainly, that's not how it *is.*" Aunt Clare blew her nose and finished with a hopeful, "Is it?"

Mel laughed. "Tony is a wonderful husband, thank you. Not perfect, nobody's perfect, but I'm happy."

"I'm the insurance policy," I said. Mel ignored me, and I ignored the interested look on the grandmother's face as she came back with the bread and mayo, and sat down.

I lifted half my sandwich off the plate in front of Kerrie and took a bite. The grandmother took a bite of hers, shooting me a look that said there were *some* sensible people in the room. I liked being included in that look.

The puppy yelped with fresh determination. We silently agreed to ignore it. I took another bite of my half a sandwich.

Aunt Clare said, "When I think back, I remember being so full of promise."

"Give me a for instance, " Mel said, sitting down with a plateful of fried bologna to be made into sandwiches. I got busy spreading mayo on bread.

"When I was in Brownies, I sold more Girl Scout cookies than any other Brownie in the entire state of Tennessee," Aunt Clare was saying. "They gave me an award, do you remember?"

"Vaguely," Mel said.

"I can show it to you," she said almost eagerly.

"That's all right," Mel said, waving away this offer.

Aunt Clare said, "It hangs next to my fireplace."

"Then I doubt I'll miss it," Mel said.

"I just stepped up to people's doors. People I'd never met before and might never meet again," Aunt Clare said, with something like wonder. "And I'd offer them a wide grin and a sunny personality, and they would order just boxes and boxes of cookies."

"Well, good for you," Mel said irritably.

"The point is," Aunt Clare said with exaggerated patience, "I used to be this little girl everybody loved. Something just shifted for me, the stars, or the plates of the earth, or some mysterious something. People don't just automatically like me anymore."

Kerrie looked at me for a lead. I gave her back a tiny shrug.

"There are plenty of people who like you," the grandmother said. "Not that you ought to be knocking on doors, of course, but you just need to be more outgoing."

"I used to be," Aunt Clare said. "I used to think I had reason to be confident, but things have changed since my husband left me. Even my most recent closest friend told me, when she first met me a question popped right into her head: Do I really like this woman?"

Mel laughed out loud.

"That was not meant to be funny, Melisande."

"Maybe not, but it was. This new friend of yours, she likes you fine now, doesn't she?"

"It's only been three months."

"She trusts you enough to be honest with you, isn't that enough? Did she have to love you at first sight?"

"Since you put it that way . . ."

"You're too hard on people, Clare. But you're even harder on yourself."

"That's the nicest thing you've ever said to me, Melisande," Aunt Clare said in sincere tones.

We'd all been ignoring the puppy's whining, but it was getting to me. Now the creature burst into a frenzy of resentment, barking and crying and whining all being brought into play. This went on for about twenty seconds and then stopped abruptly.

Kerrie started out of her chair, but Mel pointed at her, very master of our ship, and Kerrie sat back down. Mel went to peek out the door. "It's fine," she said, coming back to the table. "It's safe. If you let it see you and then go away again, it'll only feel worse. So eat, and then you can go out and pet it."

"I really want this dog," Kerrie said.

The puppy broke a single tortured bark that came in two voices, like something out of a scary movie. But it didn't sound scary, just miserable. And then nothing. We chewed with an air of waiting for the next round.

"That's how our other dog sounded when he didn't

wake up one morning," Kerrie said as she finished off the half sandwich. "Quiet."

"Elvira, go take a walk," Mel said. "Take Kerrie with you."

"Are you going to decide about the puppy?" she asked, making the most of the babyish voice she'd adopted lately. "While we're out, I mean."

"I'm not promising a thing, Kerrie," Mel said, "except that if you throw yourself on the floor again, I am going to put you up for adoption."

"I'll take her," Aunt Clare said.

"You can't have her," Mel said. "I'll only let mean people take her."

Chapter 15

"LET'S PLAY that game again," Kerrie said as we went down the front steps.

"What game is that?"

"Where you tell me the police want me for murder. That was fun."

"That was no game," I said. "I thought I scared you to death."

She laughed. Not a ha-ha-on-you kind of laugh, but a thoroughly delighted laugh that meant big sisters were so silly or—well, I don't know what it meant, but it was not the reaction I was going for.

"Weren't you worried?"

"About what? The death sentence? I'm eight years old, for Pete's sake."

"Go play by yourself. You're too old for me."

"I'm going to be nicer to him than you are to me," she said.

"Him who?"

"Our baby brother."

"How do you know it's a brother?"

"It is. He is. I just know," she said, going off by herself to I didn't know where. "You'll see," she said over her shoulder. "I'm going to be so nice to him, he'll love me way better than he loves you."

I didn't doubt this was true. I thought I wouldn't care. But I did.

I cared a lot.

I followed Kerrie for five minutes in one direction, then we turned around and went back. Aunt Clare had the sleeping puppy draped over her lap, but Kerrie pretended not to notice. I decided she was smarter than I thought.

"It wouldn't do to send you off to a motel," the grandmother was saying.

"We don't mind motels, Momma," Mel said. "I told you that already."

"They never wash the bedspreads in them motels," the grandmother said.

"I saw that program too," Mel said. "I thought about buying these silk bed sacks that you slip between the sheets so you never really have to touch the pillows or any of the bedclothes."

Aunt Clare butted in here to say, "I've seen those. They

don't have a zipper up the side, that's the only trouble. You have to sort of slide down in, and I thought, what if there was a fire in the middle of the night?"

The grandmother's eyes flicked to the window and back, very quickly.

I said, "So it's settled? Do Kerrie and I sleep together, or do we each get our own room?"

The subject of fires was dropped. Also, we were staying.

We all trooped upstairs. The puppy rode in the crook of Aunt Clare's arm, like a football. A limp football. On the way up, the grandmother warned us that these rooms were bound to be needing some work.

Kerrie's room was pink. "This used to be my room," Aunt Clare said. This I could believe. It had cheerleader and prom queen written all over it, in ruffles.

Aunt Clare began the tour with the words, "Do you know how to twirl a baton?" and Kerrie was hooked.

Mel looked into what I knew had to have been her old room just from the way she moved toward it, as if she were about to peer into a dollhouse.

But then she straightened; her whole posture told me the room had changed a lot. Mel's voice came high-pitched when she said, "Why, Momma, do you still sew?"

The grandmother hurried over to share the doorway. "It's a terrible trouble to keep setting up the machine and taking it away. And then I had it in the dining room, but it's just too dark in there to suit me."

Standing right behind the grandmother, I saw a long worktable rested within a bed's imprints in the carpeting. A smaller table with a sewing machine took up the space in front of the side-by-side windows.

The yellow paint was cheerful. The wooden dresser looked nice with the afternoon sunlight hitting it. In the middle of the room, I turned in a circle, looking around.

"I had your bed moved across the hall from my sister's room only a few weeks ago," the grandmother said in an apologetic tone. "I didn't know you'd be coming home, or I would have waited."

"Don't worry about it, Momma." Mel sounded impatient. She probably felt too flattened to lift her mood just enough to satisfy the grandmother that she wasn't heartbroken.

I personally thought Mel's heart had broken just a little.

Maybe the grandmother thought so too, because she said, "I thought I'd make myself some kitchen curtains."

"That's a fine idea." Still flattened.

"I need sunlight to thread a needle these days," the grandmother said. "And there's a good view of my neighbor's flower garden."

"Don't apologize, Momma. I'm just tired to death," Mel said.

"Are you sure?"

"I'm sure," Mel said.

"You can sleep in your own bed, anyway," the grandmother

said, leading us on to that room. Here, Mel made more of an effort. She sat down hard and fell back on the bed like this was it for her, don't bother her till morning.

My room was the best. The grandmother was right, this side of the house lacked for sun. But there was a tree right outside the windows, and because they were open by about three inches at the bottom, bird chatter filled the room.

The rest of the view was of a garage off to one side of the backyard, and behind it there seemed to be a garden. The garage sat where the greenhouse could be found in our yard, and Mel's veggie garden back of it. It was not home, but had the pattern of home and felt right to me.

"This was my sister's bedroom," the grandmother said. "When she passed, it lay empty until I got married. Then we started calling it the guest room."

It was green, mostly. A faded green rug and an uphol-stered chair, walls gone creamy with age. The bed was covered with a quilt. In the books I read, the best grand-mothers always had quilts.

"We'll find the curtains for this room," the grand-mother said. "I hardly ever come upstairs anymore, and it's going to pot."

"It's nice without," I said, going to the bookcase. There were old books here; I'd seen these titles at flea markets. *The Bobbsey Twins. Five Little Peppers and How They Grew.* "I like this room the way it is."

"Fold up this quilt, will you?" she went on, still not looking at me. "We'll find you fresh linens."

"I get to use the quilt, though, don't I? After we change the sheets?"

"Only if we wash it. I can't have your mother wishing she'd bought those silk bed sacks after all."

We legged all the bed linens down to the "warshing pantry." Even Kerrie, who had more sheet trailing behind her than she had in her arms. We left Aunt Clare with Mel to sort out the suitcase she shared with Kerrie.

The grandmother began once more to tell us her story about the iron as we approached the pantry, how she set up the ironing board too near the window. "It was the curtains again. Curtains are a terrible hazard."

I thought she sounded a little nervous. When she opened the door, I was looking right at what I suspected was the trunk of the tree that reached my bedroom window. Behind it, I could see the back doors of two houses at the other side of the block.

"Big hole," I said. It was a shock, but mainly I was impressed. "It must've been some fire."

"Not really," she said. "The firemen knocked the wall out. Just took their axes to it, can you imagine?"

I didn't have to imagine it. The broken edges were right before me.

"The repairs ought to have been done this week," the grandmother said, flapping a hand at the hole, now covered in clear plastic. "Nobody finishes a job on time these days."

"It'll be good as new," I said, but I couldn't sound convinced. In the kitchen, it looked like they'd popped a new window into a window-shaped hole and that was that. This wasn't a window-shaped hole.

I could see the outside wall, the charred edges of cotton-candy insulation, and the plastered-over slats that made up the inside wall. I had no idea how somebody fixed such a mess.

The grandmother didn't look at the wall at all. "Let's drop all this laundry right here. Kerrie, have you ever helped with the wash before?"

It was a mistake to notice the hole at all, I could see that now. I was sorry about it. I wanted to say something else, turn the subject in some way so that she would forgive me, or at least forget about it. But everything I thought of didn't sound right.

"Now let's sort out the whites, Kerrie," the grand-mother said.

Pretty much ignoring me.

"If Daddy was here," I said, "he'd know what needs to be done. No big deal, really."

"Elvira, would you give the rooms upstairs a good vac-uuming and do a little dusting? Open the windows," the grandmother said. "The vacuum is in the hall closet."

Chapter 16

THE VACUUM cleaner was one of those old-fashioned standing ones that can be practically raced from room to room. I raced it. *Stupid, stupid, stupid,* I kept saying to myself.

When I turned the vacuum off, I heard Mel and Aunt Clare in my room, talking. I could hear everything they said. Not that they talked so loudly, but I did my best dusting close by the open door.

Aunt Clare said, "I think the time has come to talk about a nursing home."

"For Momma? Because she left her iron on?"

"Because she nearly burned the whole house down," Aunt Clare said. "Three times."

"Three? The window in the kitchen and the laundry room fire and what else?"

"She decided to burn fallen leaves and burned down the garden shed."

"She mentioned that," Mel said.

"She's just not facing facts," Aunt Clare said. "The wind got hold of the fire and blew it thataway, is all she will admit to."

"It happens."

"The fire could just as easily have blown toward the house, Melisande. At the time, I was only concerned that she let that fire get out of control. That she didn't keep the hose right next to her. But then her backyard neighbor told me she went around to the other side of the house to prune some bushes. She wasn't tending the fire at all like she claimed."

"She made a mistake," Mel said. "But you can't count the fan, it could have happened to anyone."

"Who do you know that it happened to?"

"We'll just get her an iron with automatic shutoff," Mel said. "The woman is sharp as a tack, Clare. She doesn't belong in a nursing home."

"The only sharp left to her is on her tongue, Melisande." Aunt Clare was spitting the words out. "She went to the library one day and decided to leave her car parked there in the lot while she walked around to the corner drugstore. When she came back out, Momma looked up and down the street for the car and she thought it had been stolen. Reported it to the police."

"Anybody could—"

"Forget where she parked her car? For a moment or two, yes. For five minutes, even. But to fill out a police report and call me to come bring her home and *still* not remember? The point is, she forgets things now. She makes mistakes that could get her hurt, or worse."

While I listened, I held the picture of that hole in the wall in my mind. I didn't know what to think.

Mel said, "I see how upset you are, Clare. But I've only been here a few hours. I need a little longer to get a sense of how Momma's doing."

"She's losing it," Aunt Clare shouted. Then said, "Shhh," like it was Mel who'd done the shouting. Her voice was lowered when she added, "Can't you take my word for it?"

I went to stand in the doorway as Mel said, "I guess not. What did you mean, anyway, leaving me that message, 'Momma's time has come'?"

"I don't remember what I said on the message," Aunt Clare said. "Just whatever came to mind."

"Well, maybe we ought to put *you* in the nursing home." Mel's breath chopped up her voice as she lifted one corner of the mattress to fold the sheet under it. Aunt Clare didn't make a move to help her.

I took over the job, and Mel stood away to face Clare with her hands on her hips. Her fighting stance. "For heaven's sake, Clare, I thought she was dying. I thought I'd missed my chance to make up with her."

"Is that what you're doing here? Making up with her?"

"You make it sound like I'm plotting against you, Clare. Just remember I wouldn't be here now if you hadn't called."

"I know that. Don't you think I know that?" Aunt Clare said. "But I didn't expect you to side with Momma against me."

"Clare . . ." Mel sat down on the bed, which interfered only a little with folding the top sheet back. "Oh, I don't know. I haven't seen her forget anything just yet."

"How long are you planning to stay?"

"What?" Sleepless Mel didn't seem to be quite a match for Memphis Barbie.

"It might be weeks before she does something more to endanger herself or the neighborhood—"

"The neighborhood?" Mel looked like she was tempted to laugh. "Are you exaggerating just a little?"

Clare lost her temper. "Does Elvira *have* to stand right there and listen to everything we say?"

This I ignored. I was shaking pillows into faded lavender cases, I was busy. Mel said, "She might as well know why we're here."

"Obviously I cannot reason with you. Why should anything be different, even after all these years?"

"I don't know," Mel said, just as stubbornly.

"I shouldn't be one bit amazed," Aunt Clare said, leaning over to shake her finger in Mel's face. "You were never the right kind of sister to me. You always acted like you hoped something dreadful would happen to me."

"Not dreadful," Mel said, her voice shrill, her eyes wide. "I just wished you'd disappear."

"Oh, that's not too dreadful."

Mel brought her voice down to normal and somewhat sarcastic to say, "Well, I didn't wish it all the time, Clare. Just whenever it was inconvenient to have a little sister." But then she lost it again, standing up as near to Aunt Clare as the Belly would let her get. "Do you remember my one and only slumber party?"

"Do I? You wouldn't let me come. You and your friends shut your bedroom door in my face," Aunt Clare yelled.

"We must be remembering a different party," Mel said right back, really and truly worked up now.

"You might want to hold it down," I said. The last thing we needed here was a knock-down, drag-out fight. But Mel was rolling.

"You crashed the one I remember," she said. "And after giving me your solemn promise you would watch TV with Momma and Daddy."

"I just wanted to be with all of you," Aunt Clare whined.

"You were. Those girls spent hours curling your hair and painting your face."

"I had the best time."

"See, you do remember," Mel said furiously. "But it was my party and I wanted it all to myself."

"You were mean to me."

"I just wanted to have one night," Mel said, and repeated it more loudly. "*One night* to be the way it would have been if I'd never had a little sister."

"That's mean." Aunt Clare looked at me. "Don't you think that's mean?" To put a stop to this, I had to agree with her. But really, I knew just how Mel felt.

Kerrie and the grandmother could be heard coming up the stairs, which forced a lull in the combat. They brought in a fresh load of sheets. "Smell," Kerrie said, pushing the sheets into Mel's face. "Springtime freshness."

"Wonderful," Mel said, going pale. "Let me help you make your bed."

"No, no," the grandmother said. "Kerrie and I can manage. You all did enough."

Aunt Clare said she had to be getting on to feed the puppies. I figured she had a team of elves to handle the hard labor at home, since she didn't appear to be one for stepping up to help. But likely those elves needed constant supervision.

Kerrie and I were given hot chocolate and cinnamon toast for an early supper and sent to bed before it was really dark. Neither Kerrie nor I fought it. I didn't know how long Mel planned to stay, but I wanted to lie awake and enjoy having my own room.

I rested one arm on the table and leaned into it, looking forward to lying awake all through dusk and then being in the dark for at least an hour. I wanted to breathe in the smells of the grandmother's home. Part old wood and lemon oil, part books and cinnamon.

I wanted to think about spending the night in the grandmother's house. My grandmother. I wanted to get used to the idea. Then I wanted to figure out how to make the grandmother like me. Step 1: Don't comment on the size of the hole she burns into anything.

Like the very thought was a cue, Mel got up from the table, saying, "I'll check the dryer."

I got up fast. "I'll check it. The quilt is for me."

I got there first, but Mel followed me, saying, "I didn't know you liked quilts so much. You never show any interest in them at flea markets."

I tried to get in and out of the laundry room fast, but it was hard to get that quilt to pop right out of the dryer. It was still wet in the center, so I turned the wet side out and shoved it back in.

By then Mel had come to stand in the doorway. She stared at the plastic covering on the wall. At the hole. "You know, it looked a little bigger to me the first time I was in here," I said. "Once the surprise wears off, it doesn't make you want to go, 'Oh, wow.'"

The grandmother showed up behind Mel. She said, "What are you thinking?" and Mel said, "That children are a constant amazement."

Good answer.

"The quilt is still wet," I said, standing in front of them

like a dog who wanted to be let out. It was how I felt, really. "I'm going upstairs to unpack my stuff, if that's okay."

"Be my guest," the grandmother said, but not in quite the dry tone she'd used to not quite welcome us in. I figured we were like the hole in the wall. Once she was over the first shock of us, it was okay that we were here.

In my room, I opened a dresser drawer. I hoped to find one empty so I could put my clothes away and feel like a regular granddaughter must feel, visiting Grandma. Even if it was only for a day or so.

There was a smell, the exact rich woodsy smell I was expecting. And there were a lot of loose photos in the drawer. Most of the ones right on top were of Kerrie and me. These were the ones Mel sent at Christmas. I shut the drawer, not sure how to feel about any of this.

I did feel something, neither sad nor happy. It was too much like the feeling of being in trouble to call it excitement. I got into bed, putting that drawer at the back of my mind like a book I was not ready to read.

Mel came to look in on me. "You were awfully quiet the last half hour or so. Is something bothering you?"

"I didn't know you were writing to her. Your mother. I thought you weren't talking to her at all. Except for the Christmas cards."

"I didn't write letters in the sense that you're talking about. Starting 'Dear Momma' and ending 'Love, Mel.' I sent reports."

"Reports?"

"I let her know when we moved, when I got pregnant, when I had a baby. When we settled down, I wrote her your daddy was going into business."

"Did she write back?"

"Now and then. I called her when your other grand-momma died. She had just broken her foot or she would have come to the funeral. Aunt Clare came, though, do you remember?"

I shook my head. Those few days of going to the funeral home were just a memory of rain hitting the windshield for what seemed like a very long time.

"It's just not right," I said, "that I didn't know more about her." This much I knew was true, but I couldn't think exactly how Mel might have done differently.

"She can be so stubborn. Was *being* stubborn. I just didn't want you to hope for something that might not happen. Like having another grandmother."

I thought of the pictures, stuffed into a drawer in this room that had belonged to someone who died. I said, "I still don't know if that will happen."

"Why, Elvira," Mel said. "It already has."

Maybe. But I wasn't sure.

"Was Aunt Clare this mean to you when she was Kerrie's age and you were mine?"

"I don't suppose so," Mel said, and then double-clutched. "Not that she's being mean now, it's just that we have a lot of stuff to work out. Old stuff we never really talked through."

"I know that's the right answer to give," I said. "But I want you to really think about it and tell me the truth, even if it isn't pretty."

"Why are you asking this?"

"I sure hope Kerrie isn't going to grow up to be such a pain in the neck. She is one, of course. Right now. But I had hopes she'd improve."

"Then I have to say you're asking the wrong question," Mel said. "I think you should ask was I nicer to Clare when we were kids."

I sank into the pillows with a groan.

"Right now, it sounds like Clare feels all used up," Mel said.

"Let's don't talk about her anymore tonight."

Mel patted me on the butt and was gone. I couldn't tell if she crept back downstairs or went off to bed. When I turned out the lamp, I flipped onto my side, the way I like to sleep.

The window screen was aglow with moving green lights. Flickering green lights that after the first startled moment I realized were fireflies.

I didn't last long enough to know how long they stayed.

Chapter 17

MEL HAD already eaten breakfast with the grandmother by the time I rolled out of bed at ten-thirty. "We're going to paint the window," the grandmother announced, like she was telling me we were going to the zoo.

"Hoo-ray," I muttered under my breath. I am not human when I first get up, no matter how late. I headed straight for the coffeepot and nobody said a word. Chocolate donuts had come from somewhere, and I greeted them like gifts from the tooth fairy.

"Maybe we'll paint the whole kitchen," Mel said. "We'll take your car, Momma, to go downtown and buy some paint."

Now that I had a mouthful of chocolate, I didn't mind.

The grandmother went upstairs to put on a going-to-town dress. Mel and I were alone.

"When was Daddy supposed to come home?"

"Things won't even heat up till tomorrow night. He went early so he could catch up with some old friends. Put out feelers for a job out there."

"A job? He's planning to move out there?" The shock all but took my breath away.

"We're going to have to move unless we're expecting this child to sleep with us until you go off to college. We can't add an ant farm to that room you and Kerrie share."

Too true. At least she was still talking like we were all going to be living together. "I thought you meant we were moving to a bigger house in town," I said.

"Me too," Mel said. "I just didn't know how serious your daddy was about this Vegas thing till last week."

"I wish we could talk to him," I said.

Mel didn't say anything. Kerrie was coming downstairs. She had been up and dressed for some time, judging from Mel's reaction as she came into the kitchen. "You changed clothes again?"

She held out the skirt of a dress with a ruffled hem and twirled. "I don't have anything else to do," she said.

Aunt Clare came in the back door, unannounced even by the sound of her footsteps. "Where's Momma?"

"Upstairs," Kerrie said.

Aunt Clare said, "Have you given any thought to what we talked about?" Pretty much putting Mel on the spot.

"We still don't have enough room for that dog," I said.

I got a look loaded with the message that Aunt Clare

was not warming to me. But then the grandmother could be heard on the stairs and we all went silent.

Aunt Clare reached for a mug and poured herself a coffee.

Kerrie said, "Why's it so quiet in here?"

"No one wants to upset you over the dog," I said as the grandmother came in.

She took one look at Kerrie and broke into a smile. So Kerrie didn't give the dog another thought. She did her little dance routine for the grandmother.

The grandmother was pretty nicely turned out herself. The dress she wore clung to her till she moved, and then it sort of floated around her. I particularly admired her hairdo, swept up in a kind of roll at the back of her head. She looked old and wrinkled, of course, but she was pretty too.

Mel stood up and I saw she'd put on her one and only maternity skirt instead of those knit pants with the elastic waist. Standing there in jeans and a vintage Jimi Hendrix T-shirt with one tiny hole in the rib cage area plus a few donut crumbs, I asked myself, What's wrong with this picture?

The grandmother asked, "This is how you go to town?"

"I didn't know we were going to town. I didn't bring any dresses," I said, leaving out the information that I didn't own one at the moment. That I likely wouldn't own one until someone died or got married.

"Momma, don't make this about respect," Mel said. "We're going to buy paint."

The grandmother gave a little sniff and turned away.

Just then the doorbell rang. Kerrie and I followed her to the door, me brushing away donut crumbs. We opened the door to find that elderly gentleman with singed eyebrows standing there.

He wore a different golf pro outfit today; the blue collar and short-sleeved cuffs of the white shirt matched his pants. "Good morning, Vertie," he said. "Won't you introduce me to these lovely girls?"

The grandmother blushed. "It's just we've had some catching up to do."

"I'm Mr. Singer," he told us. "Abe Singer." He made the *g* sound hard, like the beginning of a new word.

When he stayed on for coffee and donuts, Mel excused herself to go buy some gas for the car. I was just squirting Hershey's syrup into a cup of coffee for myself. But I said, "Want me to come along?"

Mel grinned and said, "I just need ten minutes alone."

The grandmother told Mr. Singer all about my wall-washing talents and Kerrie's abilities with a load of wash, and he didn't sound like he was faking his interest in this information. Little muscles moved his few remaining eyebrow hairs around almost constantly as he listened. He was an easy fellow to like.

Aunt Clare showed off her glitter manicure and Kerrie's.

"I have jobs at home, too," Kerrie told him, going back to a subject with a little more mileage in it. "I turn the grow lights on in the basement in the morning and turn them off when it starts to get dark. That's the easy one."

"So then, you're not just a pretty face," he said to make Kerrie smile.

Aunt Clare said, "The little sisters are always the glamour girls."

This stung me badly, and even Kerrie glanced at me for some hint about how she ought to respond. The grandmother was putting cat food into a dish, same as yesterday. But she looked over, frowning.

"I didn't mean that to sound like a dig," Aunt Clare said when the moment stretched. "Elvira has that wonderful tall gangly look that models are made of, anybody can see that. Nobody is more glamorous than models, except maybe actresses."

I said, "Thank you, Aunt Clare."

"I didn't mean to hurt your feelings, sweetie," she said with real feeling. "You're just going through that stage girls go through. You'll wake up one morning wanting to try a little harder, you'll see."

"Put a sock in it, Clare," the grandmother said.

"Why, Momma—"

Mr. Singer pointed to my feet and said, "I've been admiring your Birkenstocks." I put out a coy foot, the way a model would.

"Those things have a name?" the grandmother said, but not unkindly. It was more a statement of disbelief.

"These are Mel's," I said. "Lately, her feet swell and the strap rubs up a blister, so I have them on loan."

Mr. Singer said he used to buy himself Birkenstocks but

his son kept taking them. "Nothing to beat them for comfort," he said to the grandmother. "I have a bunion."

She said, "I might have to give them a try."

"These are size nine," I said, thinking she meant to try them on. She sat down with us, still never looking at me, unless the sandals counted.

"Why, you have small feet," she said. "I could never get into a size nine."

This made me grin.

Aunt Clare sighed, as if this talk of bunions and practical shoes had begun to tire her.

The front door opened and Mel called, "I'm back," but she went up the stairs. She was probably too embarrassed to head straight for the downstairs bathroom in front of company.

Mr. Singer said, "It's been a long time since I've seen a Fireflite. Do you think I could take a closer look?"

"Let's go kick the tires," the grandmother said. I walked as far as the front porch with them, answering Mr. Singer's questions the way I'd heard Daddy do for people a hundred times.

I stopped at the swing, and the grandmother took him out to see the car her very own self, looking like it was a matter of some pride to her. He kept a guarding hand near the small of her back as they went down the stairs, although he never touched her. Never made her feel she needed his aid.

And in fact she was a head taller than he was—maybe she should have been more watchful of *him*.

Chapter 18

WHEN MEL came downstairs, I said, "I think Mr. Singer likes the grandmother."

"I think so too," Mel said, and watched them through the screen door for a minute. She liked what she saw.

Kerrie and I got the backseat. Mel drove. The grandmother said she didn't really care to. She watched out the window, saying, "Turn left here, right here," and talked about whatever she thought would be of interest to Mel. Who was married or divorced. Which of her school friends had come back to Memphis. Even which one of them had gone missing while rock climbing in Alaska.

On one corner, a fenced-in yard was chock-full of junk on tables.

"Let's stop here at this yard sale," the grandmother said.

Mel slowed down. "Anything special you want to look for?"

"I need an iron."

Mel stopped right smack in the middle of the street. "Oh, Momma, you don't want a secondhand iron. Let's go to the mall and buy you a brand-new one."

"These new irons aren't heavy enough. I want an old iron, nice and heavy, so I don't have to push down so hard."

"Well, that's a consideration," Mel said, craning her neck as if she would be able to lay her eyes on the iron if it was there.

Someone came up behind us and laid on the horn. Mel moved along, deciding not to do the yard sale after all. The grandmother didn't argue with this, but said, "I like to shop in the old part of town. I find everything I need, and the shops know me. Nobody knows their customers in the mall."

"I'll go anywhere you want," Mel said. "The main thing is, the iron should be new."

"You've been talking to Clare."

"Yes, well, she's worried about you. We both are."

"You both have worries enough without worrying about me," the grandmother said. "I think I'm going to sell the house."

Mel looked shocked. "Why would you do that, Momma?"

"I'm getting too old to manage it. You see how I live. Ignoring most of the upstairs. Even the rooms I spend my time in haven't seen a dust cloth in a month or more."

"There are times when I can say the same about mine," Mel said, "and I have child labor to fall back on. You just have other priorities right now, Momma."

"She has a boyfriend," I said, making the grandmother gasp.

Mel shot me a look through the rearview mirror—a twinkling of her eyes—but she had seen the hole in the washing pantry wall, and while she said nothing, she must have been thinking about it.

We drove through an older part of town, kind of funky, like the whole place had been found at a flea market. I spotted a pizza place offering an Elvis karaoke night. Another few blocks and the neighborhood started to improve.

Mel remembered a few places that used to be there, and the grandmother acted like she was giving a guided tour. "Now this area got a little run-down for a time," she said, "but lately it's been gussied up. I do like meandering through here of an afternoon."

I was glad the hardware store turned out to be only a couple of blocks away. We drove around the block twice, looking for a parking space nearby. A shop caught my eye, Pandora's Tattoo and Piercing Parlor. The window was hung with beads of all colors and there were little pictures of the tattoos people could get, I guess.

I didn't point the place out to anyone. I wasn't even sure why it interested me. Just around the corner, the hardware store looked old beyond belief. Like it was part of a movie set or something.

We parked, and the four of us filed into the hardware store. It was everything the look of it promised to be. Bare wood floors needing the attention of a broom and then some varnish. Shelves full of cardboard boxes of nails and screws, garden gloves hung from pegboard. Rows of wooden drawers filled with all types and sizes of drawer knobs and hinges and I don't know what all.

Nobody told us not to touch anything. In fact, there didn't look to be anybody in the place but a few other shoppers. The cash register was way in the back of the store, like the owner had never heard of shoplifters.

But the rows of appliances, also found in back, rivaled the ones in any department store. We picked through the irons, weighing the boxes in our hands. Nothing suited the grandmother.

"You know, we might get some solder and stick some lead weights onto the sides of an iron," Mel said.

"Do you mean welding?" the grandmother said, like a lightbulb went on over her head.

"Yes, but nothing fancy," Mel said. "Your iron won't look so pretty when we're done."

"Who needs an iron to be pretty?" The grandmother picked one out.

The paints were in another aisle. Mel and the grandmother started to go through the different little booklets of color chips, showing each other white. Always white.

Kerrie looked bored too. "How many whites are there?"

"Pearls, snowflakes, roses," the grandmother said. "Salt, the bottoms of my feet, drowned earthworms."

"Euww," Kerrie said, but she laughed.

"I'm going down the street for a bottle of Coke," I said.

"Take Kerrie with you."

"Aw, Mel."

"My mind can't be in two places at once, Elvira. You're right here, you can look after your sister. Then I can concentrate on paint."

I didn't bother to argue. Some battles are lost before they're begun.

"Can we have enough money for candy?" Kerrie said.

"Ease up on the sugar," the grandmother said. "You'll rot your teeth."

"I'm not worried," Mel said, handing me a five-dollar bill. "They have Tony's teeth. He's never had a cavity."

"They're buying white paint, how much concentration does that take?" I muttered as we left the store.

"You heard Aunt Clare," Kerrie said. "Mel is an older mother."

"Practically senile," I said with a laugh.

We walked to the first little grocery I could find. An old couple were running it, and there were a few shoppers who didn't look at all scary. "Look, you can buy Coke and candy in here. I'm going to give you the money and you can pick whatever you want."

Kerrie, for all of her faults, is not a dimwit. "And while

I'm rotting my teeth, where are you going to be?" she asked, tucking the bill into her ruffled shoulder bag.

"I just want ten minutes alone, that's all," I said. "I'm going to the end of the block. I'll look into a couple of stores and then I'll come back for you. Don't go back to the hardware store without me. And buy yourself a Baby Ruth or something with peanuts. A little protein never hurt."

"Okay, but don't be too long. I'm not old enough to want ten minutes alone."

"You will be," I said.

"When?"

"In about two months, after the baby comes."

Chapter 19

I COULDN'T say exactly when curiosity turned into determination. I only know I didn't waste time studying the pictures of tattoos taped to the windows. I went right in.

There was a blackboard menu on the wall; all the prices were up there. The money I brought from home would cover it. The trip to Blue Moody's would have to wait another couple of weeks, that's all.

A guy with several tattoos perched against a stool, reading a newspaper spread over a glass showcase. He wore a bandanna that hid his hair, but he looked clean. In a firm, businesslike voice, I said, "Is Pandora here?"

"That would be me, hon," he said with a quirky little grin. I waited to see if he was going to raise the parental consent issue. If he did, Kerrie wasn't going to have to worry about ten minutes alone.

But when he got off the stool, I was half a head taller than he was, and that seemed to tip the balance in my favor. I leaned over the counter and looked at his fingernails. Clean.

"I'd like to wear three little hoop earrings on this ear," I told him. I pointed out the hoops in the case.

"You have any other sites in mind?" he asked.

"Other sites?"

"Other ear?"

"Oh. No."

"Nose, lip, belly button?" I wasn't sure whether he was asking or suggesting.

"No, no, and no."

"I have a client with webbed toes. She had studs put between her toes," he said. But he didn't seem to be trying to sell me on the idea.

"Like a duck, webbed toes?"

"Right, like a duck."

I felt my stomach turn right over, the way Mel was always talking about. "I'm sure it's an interesting subject, but that's already more than I want to know."

"Okay, so where do you want the first hole?" He picked up a pen to mark my ear.

"Here, here, and here. You think that's the right distance apart?"

"Yeah, that's good. But I don't recommend multiple piercings in the same general area in a single appointment."

"Why not?"

He shrugged. "Swelling. If you had other sites in mind, we could work on those in the same appointment."

I considered letting him in on the fact I'd likely be locked in a dungeon for the next year, but that would be telling.

"Swelling, but not infection?" I didn't, after all, care to have my ear amputated later in the week.

"Nobody gets infected from my work," he said in an offended tone. "I'm a professional."

"See, the thing is, I don't live in Memphis. And I can't get this done, you know, professionally, where I do live. So this is pretty much my only shot."

"Uh-*huh,*" he said, as if I'd handed him his first algebra problem.

"If you could tell me what to do to reduce the swelling, if I should take aspirin, like that. I can take the temporary discomfort."

"Temporary discomfort." I liked that.

"Well, ice for swelling, of course. Aspirin, that's okay. You got to clean the holes with alcohol, and you can put it in the fridge, that will help kill the pain. Don't shampoo for a few days either."

Pain? "Pain? Or temporary discomfort?"

"Minor pain," he said confidently. "You can take it."

I pushed away the thought of pain and novocaine.

"Are there any health issues around this? You use clean needles, right?"

"I don't use an ear punch, don't worry. Disposable needles. No problem. There isn't usually any blood."

"What about acupuncture meridians?" I remembered reading that the ear had a site for every organ in the body. What if I punched a kidney or something? My spleen. My heart?

"I haven't had any complaints."

"So. Really. How much is this going to hurt?"

It wasn't so bad, really. He numbed the skin, and except for a pinprick and then a feeling like he kept pressing on that spot, the ear felt nothing.

By the time I was paying for the piercing and the earrings, I had this horrible sense of having made a really big mistake. I started to worry that I had left Kerrie for too long. What if she had tried to go back to Mel on her own and got lost?

No, that was stupid, we'd only turned a corner. But what if she'd made it back and told them I'd gone off and left her? Mel would kill me, that's what.

Who was I kidding? Mel was going to kill me anyway. Which might not be an entirely bad thing. The numbness had begun to wear off by the time I was shutting one shop door, and the whole left side of my head was throbbing like a drum by the time I opened the next one.

"Kerrie?" I sounded like I was dying. I tried again, speaking from deep in my belly. "Kerrie?" I still sounded like I was dying, but this time I sounded like I could deal with it.

"Right here," she said from behind a rack of comics. "Have you got any more money?"

"For what?"

She went right into whiny mode. "I found a whole bunch of great comics and I forgot to bring any from ho-ome. I don't have anything to ree-ead."

I dug my last few dollars out of my pocket and handed them to her. "Here you go. Knock yourself out."

She gave me an odd look. "What's the matter with you?"

"I have a headache. No, an earache."

But once the words were out, I realized I did have a headache. A real monster of a headache. By then Kerrie'd gotten a better look at my ear and figured things out for herself.

I leaned my forehead on the glass pane of the door and waited while Kerrie bought her comic books. It was not actually cooling, but it helped me hold my head up.

"Here, I got you some aspirin," she said, handing me a little flat tin box. "And the guy says you can get some water in the back, so we don't have to buy a drink. Which is good, because I used up every last penny we had. Actually, I still owe him three cents."

"Water's fine," I said. "Thanks for the aspirin."

"Come on, take one. Then let's get back there before they decide to paint another room."

I took three aspirin.

While I did, Kerrie tapped a fingernail against her front

teeth, thinking. I hoped she was thinking of something else that would help.

When I put the paper cup in the garbage can, she said, "Mel's gonna kill you for getting your ears pierced, and the whole paint job's going to fall on me."

That about summed up her thinking.

Chapter 20

"ONE EAR," I told Kerrie as we walked back to the hardware store. My whole head on that side felt heavy, real heavy. "I just got one ear pierced."

"Oh, very cool," she said, sounding like she was the big sister and I was the dumb kid. I wanted to hate her, I really did. I just didn't have the strength for it. I decided never to speak to her again in my whole life. At least not until I was as old as Mel.

Right before we went back into the hardware store, Kerrie tapped me on the arm. "They look really good," she said. "It will turn out to be worth it."

"You're sure?" I was really glad she reminded me of that. I couldn't help wanting to hear it again.

"Absolutely."

Pandora had told me to keep my hair away from my ear to reduce the chance of infection. But now I was more concerned about living through the day. I smoothed my hair over my ear before we went back to the paint aisle.

Mel zeroed right in on the misery on my face. "Are you feeling all right, Elvira?"

"Headache."

"She took an aspirin," Kerrie said. "What color white did you buy?"

"Almond," Mel said.

"Sounds better than drowned earthworms," Kerrie said.

"Is that why you're holding your head to one side?" the grandmother asked. "Because you have a headache?"

I straightened up, afraid the earrings would show. It occurred to me now, too late, that I'd rather Mel didn't kill me in front of the grandmother.

"I'm going to go sit in the car, okay?"

Mel handed me the keys. "But don't leave the car running. Open the windows. We won't be long, I promise."

"I'm going to go with her," Kerrie said. "I can look after her."

"Good idea, sweetie," Mel said.

"I hope I'm not going to be sorry about this," I said once we were outside.

"You will be," Kerrie said. "But not forever."

"Thanks for the thought."

We had just about eased onto the hot car seats when they came out of the store. The grandmother was quizzing

Mel on her welding skills as they got into the car, which kept Mel's mind off me.

Maybe she didn't even notice the Elvis impersonator as we drove by. He had the hair and a certain posture that I recognized. Even though he was only sitting on his front steps, tuning his guitar. Mel didn't act like she spotted him, but then Kerrie didn't say a word either, just glanced over to be sure I hadn't missed him.

We took the long way back so the grandmother could stop in at a farm stand for tomatoes. I said I'd wait in the car, and Kerrie didn't get out either.

"You want to rest your head in my lap?" she asked. "The way you did for me that time I had stitches in my knee and the novocaine wore off and it still hurt?"

"Never in a million years," I said.

But that was how I made the rest of the trip. Kerrie patted me on the shoulder steadily. There have been rare few times for Kerrie to feel called upon to think of anyone but herself, but she was showing a talent for it. I didn't even want to hate her.

"I think you ought to go take a nap," Mel said as we got out of the car. "You must be coming down with something."

She reached out to smooth my hair, that thing she does when she wants us to feel better. I didn't see it coming. Her hand brushed my ear and I pulled away with a yelp.

"What have you done?" she cried, suspicious now and all sympathy gone. I pulled my hair back for her to see. She would have to know sometime.

"Omilord," Mel cried, falling back against the grandmother. "She's maimed for life."

"Let's get inside if we're going to have a family fight," the grandmother said, leading us away from her car. "My neighbors are elderly. They can't take the stimulation."

Mel ignored this. "Where were you while this was going on?" she asked Kerrie, as if she ought to be held responsible.

Before Kerrie could reply, Mel turned on me to say, "You left her somewhere, didn't you? Or you dragged her into one of those filthy tattoo parlors. Which is it?"

One had to be worse than the other, but I was hurting too much to know what my answer should be.

"I was perfectly safe," Kerrie said. "I waited at the newsstand with a nice older couple."

"What nice couple would that be?" Mel asked snappishly as she steered me up to the porch. "Who do you two know in Memphis?"

"They owned the store," Kerrie said in the too-grownup way that could drive me crazy, but seeing it used against Mel, I loved it. "They have five grandchildren. They sell books and magazines and candy and aspirin."

Inside, Mel hurried me into the bathroom behind the kitchen. Kerrie and the grandmother trotted along behind. Mel kept up a steady patter of threat and accusation. But once we faced each other, she switched to the Mel I used to know and love. "You're so swollen," she said worriedly. "Does your ear feel hot?"

"He said I should put ice on it."

"He who? Who did this to you?" Mel wanted to know as she wet a washcloth in cold water.

"Somebody named Pandora."

"That can't be true," the grandmother said. "You said it was a man."

"She never lies," Mel said. "She just twists the truth into a pretzel."

"Thank you," I said quietly.

Mel set the chilled washcloth gently against my ear. It hurt, but it helped more. She said, "I think we could put some chipped ice in the fold of the washcloth."

"Let's do that," the grandmother said, and snatched another washcloth off the shelf before she left the bathroom.

"I'll help with the ice," Kerrie said, hot on the grandmother's heels.

"How could you do this?" Mel said. "Why did you have to do this now, of all times?"

"I don't know," I said. "I just wanted to be different somehow. I didn't really think about it a lot."

"Famous last words," Mel said.

"I didn't mean to embarrass you."

"I think you might have." She sounded resigned to the idea.

I heard the crackle of ice being freed from the tray. I had only a minute to get this over with. "I might have been doing it to embarrass Daddy."

Mel laughed.

"What's funny about that?"

"You," she said, "trying to embarrass your father, the Elvis impersonator." She shrugged. "Well, who knows? You might have hit a bull's-eye. He's a pretty conservative guy where you girls are concerned."

We heard Aunt Clare call, "Yoooo-hoo," before the back door was opened. "What are you all up to in there?" Aunt Clare asked, seeing us in the bathroom.

Mel said, "Elvira has had her ears pierced."

"Ooh, what fun," Aunt Clare said. "Let me see."

I pulled the washcloth away. "Just the one. Three times."

"It looks awful sore, but it's going to be real nice," Aunt Clare said. "Those little gold hoops are so pretty. Have you taken any cough medicine?"

Mel and I both looked at her like she'd lost her mind.

"To help the child sleep," Aunt Clare said, like she was talking to idiots. "When I had my ears done, I came home and took a sleeping pill. When I woke up, the worst was over."

"She's not taking anything to make her sleep," Mel said, sounding grim. "She can have aspirin, but otherwise she's going to suffer through it all."

The grandmother came back with the ice, offering lunch. "We should have stopped off at the grocery so we'd have something we could actually cook."

"It's too hot for that, Momma," Mel said. "It's too hot even to fry an egg."

"We've got ham and cheese for sandwiches. Mustard or mayo, what's your preference?" she asked while I switched to the washcloth with ice. It was shockingly cold, or maybe my ear was that hot, but I had to just touch the ear and lift the washcloth away.

Plus, my arm had started to get tired, like when I was braiding my hair. I put the ice against my forehead for a few seconds, and that helped a little.

"Is it yellow cheese or white?" This was Kerrie, who had apparently not been consulted while in the kitchen. "Yellow food dye isn't good for you."

"We could go out for lunch," Aunt Clare said.

"Yay," Kerrie said.

The grandmother shook her head. "We've been out. This is what came of it. Although I did get a new iron, so it isn't all a lost cause."

I wanted to point out that I was not a lost cause.

But an upset look passed over Aunt Clare's face. "I hope it has automatic shutoff," she said. There was a feeling around her of wanting to say a lot more.

"It has automatic shutoff," I said, hoping Aunt Clare did too.

Everybody trooped out of the bathroom and into the kitchen. I sat at the table, where I could rest my arm while I froze my ear. Aunt Clare threw up her hands at the idea of soldering weights to the iron.

"I'm going to go put on a housedress," the grand-mother said. "I don't want to dirty this one up in the kitchen." She had no sooner shut the door to her bedroom than Aunt Clare whispered, "I wish you hadn't bought her that iron. It only encourages her."

"In what?"

"In the belief that these fires don't change things."

"I don't know why you think Momma's going to listen to me," Mel said in a voice just above a whisper. "You were always so much closer to her. She took you on shopping trips; the two of you went to the beauty parlor."

"I know," Aunt Clare said. "I think that's the problem I'm having. You've been gone so long, she's romanticized you. Built you into the daughter you never were."

I couldn't tell if Mel had just been insulted or not. From the look on her face, I guessed she wasn't sure either. She sat down in the chair across from me, saying, "Look, Clare, all I meant was—"

"I know what you meant. When we were girls, I was Momma's favorite and you were Daddy's. It was that simple."

At this, Kerrie's eyes widened.

"No, I—" Mel got an odd look on her face. "I don't know that I'd use the word 'favorite.'"

"Well, I would," Aunt Clare said.

"All the more reason to give up the idea that I have any influence here," Mel said in a fierce whisper. "Daddy didn't have any influence with Momma when he was alive, and I don't either. I'm only staggered she isn't packing up to move into Shady Corners, if that's what you want her to do."

I thought the grandmother ought to be here. She was missing out on an important talk.

Mel said, "Have you been badgering her to sell her house?"

Right, I was thinking, *very* important talk. Miss Lasky was wrong.

"What do you want me to do, Melisande?" Aunt Clare's voice was held low, but her words came fast and angry. "Put Momma in a nursing home and run over here to vacuum on Tuesday mornings so the dust won't settle?"

"I can't help you with this, Clare." Mel got up from the table, walked toward the sink.

They might have said more, but the grandmother opened her bedroom door. Aunt Clare said, "Well, that's it, then. Let's us go to the mall, Kerrie."

"Make sure you eat," the grandmother said, coming into the kitchen. "Soon."

"No problem," Aunt Clare said. "The last thing we want is a meltdown in J. C. Penney's."

I had to admire Aunt Clare's cool. She looked and sounded like she'd been talking about nothing more upsetting than which vacuum cleaner she ought to shop for.

"Put down that washcloth for a few minutes," Mel said, "or I'm going to start worrying about frostbite."

"It's just getting numb," I said, which was fine with me.

"That's what I'm talking about. Momma and I are going outside to sit in the garden, like ladies do. Make sandwiches, would you? And bring them outside."

Mel and the grandmother spent a few minutes collecting iced tea, glasses, and napkins. Once the grandmother was sure I had paper plates and all the makings of ham-and-cheese sandwiches, I was alone in the kitchen.

My ear hurt a whole lot worse as the numbness wore off, so I spread mayo on the bread and then iced my ear for a minute. I took the wrappers off sliced cheese and then iced my ear another minute. I thought I could handle this after all.

I went over to the sink to wring out my washcloth, and while I was there, I heard them moving around under the kitchen window. The grandmother was saying, ". . . embarrassed about the baby you're carrying now?"

Mel laughed out loud. "I'm not embarrassed by this baby. Elvira might be, I suppose . . ."

There was a little bit I didn't hear clearly—a chair scraped as they settled down.

". . . get the feeling you're not real happy about it," the grandmother said.

"Sometimes I am, Momma. Other times, I ask myself, what am I starting over for? When this child is grown, I'll have spent thirty years packing school lunches, asking if the homework is done, telling somebody what time they have to be home."

The grandmother didn't reply to this. Mel went on after a few moments, saying, "I gave away all the baby stuff. Twice. Now I need to buy a crib for the third time."

"Get somebody to give you a crib. I'll give you a crib, I believe there's one in the attic."

"Some women have the good sense to get this all over with in one fell swoop—"

"And you want to be one of them?" the grandmother said, like Mel must have lost her mind. "If the other two were toddlers, I would understand perfectly. But your girls are already leaving you little by little."

"This one will do the same thing."

"Maybe you'll have a fourth," the grandmother said teasingly.

"Kids are a lot less fun as they get older," Mel said. "In fact, they're a pain in the butt. Elvira's pierced ear would be the perfect example."

I started to wish I hadn't listened in. I felt a little sick, even. Although my ear could have made me feel that way, or the aspirin. Probably three aspirin hadn't been such a good idea.

I turned to finish the sandwiches, but the grandmother stopped me with her next remark: "You hate them. The holes in her ear, I mean."

"I hate them. And Tony's going to hate them. Worse, he's going to get upset all over again every time he looks at her. We didn't need this right now."

My ear started to throb like crazy. It hurt so much, I thought I might be sick. Sweat pricked out all over me.

"Don't ever make my mistake," the grandmother said. "Don't throw the baby out with the bathwater."

"Oh," Mel said on a drawn-out sigh. "Momma."

"Don't get all soggy on me now."

I hurried over to the table, wanting to get finished so I could just sit down. I slapped the sandwiches together, put them on paper plates, and stacked these to carry them outside. By then the conversation had shifted to the problem of snails in the garden.

Chapter 21

THERE WERE three big wooden chairs set up on a little patio below the kitchen window. I said a silent hurrah for Aunt Clare. If she had stayed, she'd have taken the third chair. Kerrie and I would have had to sit in the grass, where we'd no doubt pick up bug bites and would have to spend half the night scratching.

Mel said, "Are you feeling all right, Elvira?"

"Hungry." Lie, lie, lie.

"You're awfully pale."

The grandmother said, "You'd be pale too, if you had three stab wounds."

Mel laughed out loud. "Momma!"

I managed to add to the lie with a halfhearted grin. I admit it, I wanted to impress upon the grandmother that I was a strong girl, even without ballet. At least I wanted to start winning her over, if such a thing was possible. I wanted her to look at me.

Neither one of them looked at me. They took bites of their sandwiches, admiring the clematis vine that had taken over another lawn chair, blooming in wine and deep purple.

The paint had mostly peeled off that chair, so I figured it had been a flower chair for a few summers. It was the kind of thing that looked great to me, but Daddy's customers liked a more polished look.

I put the ice up against my ear between bites. I thought I might be feeling a little bit better. Except when I thought about Daddy. It seemed like a good idea not to think about him while I was eating.

Instead, I remembered every one of Daddy's lady customers having hoop earrings or tasteful little diamond studs. Like gardens and pierced ears went together. Probably my memory was desperate to make excuses for me.

After a little more talk of snails in the garden, Mel said, "Maybe you don't need to think of selling, Momma; just hire someone to help you around the house. You've lived here since you were Kerrie's age."

"That's probably long enough, then."

I said, "I read somewhere that it's hard on older people to move to someplace new. They lose track of things, get up at night and don't remember where they are, stuff like that."

The grandmother turned a flat stare on me. "That's how you see me? As older people?"

"Older than me," I muttered, and went back to looking at the garden. So much for winning over the grandmother.

"You see?" the grandmother said. "I'm old."

"Momma."

"I'm old enough to be called an older person by my first grandbaby."

"I think that's what grandchildren are supposed to think of their grandparents. For heaven's sake, Momma, the kids think *I'm* old."

I deliberately did a wide-eyed glance-over, as if the information that Mel might not be ancient came as a real shocker. Mel was not in the least bugged; she stuck her lunchy tongue out at me.

"Gross."

The grandmother ignored all of this and said, "Your sister is afraid of getting stuck with the care of me."

"I'm not convinced you need that kind of care," Mel said.

"Then Clare has already talked to you. What did she say exactly?"

"Momma, Clare loves you—"

"I'm taking our plates inside," I said, and I did. Some things are for listening in on, and some things are meant to be private.

I got more ice for the washcloth.

I felt tight all over, the kind of tight that a shower sometimes helps. I couldn't wash my hair, but I wanted to stand under the hot water till I felt like I was melting.

I did that and then washed my hair. Very carefully, holding my head so wet hair wouldn't catch on the earrings. I stood under the hot water some more.

I'd started to worry about what if we got lucky and Daddy did come home? How mad would he be? I thought I might have to buy something tentlike to wear for the next school year to make up for it.

But I also hoped I was going to like the hoops more later, because so far they felt like a mistake. I hoped they would turn out to be cool.

As I came out of the bathroom, the grandmother was near the bottom of the staircase. I heard her saying, "I put them in the attic years ago. Which reminds me, we ought to go up there and look for that crib."

I stopped to listen.

"It's too hot for that today, Momma."

"Nonsense. If you faint, we'll simply carry you downstairs and put a cold cloth on your head."

"Give me a minute," Mel said, code for "I have to use the bathroom again."

The grandmother came up the stairs. It made her a little breathless, but she looked like she was the thing she admired: strong. She said, "Are you feeling up to a scavenger hunt?"

I nodded.

The attic stairs were behind what I thought was a closet door. The space was wide, like a regular stairway. Going into the attic felt like going into an oven, but neither one of us fainted.

"It's been taken apart," the grandmother said. "So we're watching for the ends, painted yellow. And the side rails. That's how we'll spot it." She walked one side of the attic and I walked the other, holding the washcloth to my ear, letting it drip cool water onto my shoulder.

Although my ear still throbbed, I had gotten used to it in a weird way, and it didn't make me feel like I had to lie down. "Was this Mel's crib when she was a baby?" I asked.

"Yes. Do you mind if I ask why you call your mother Mel?"

"It's what Daddy always called her," I said. "What he still calls her."

"Why do you call him Daddy, then?"

"I guess it's what Mel called him," I said. "So *I'd* know, I mean. Because he didn't always look like himself. But I think I knew anyway."

"I'm sure children can pick their own daddy out of a crowd of look-alikes."

Maybe.

Mel came upstairs, saying, "Oh, the afternoons I spent up here. But it's a lot more crowded now." She picked up a super dusty lamp shade at the top of the stairs and set it aside. "You are allowed to throw things out, Momma."

"Now don't scold," the grandmother said. "Sometimes I'm just holding on to something till I make up my mind. Then I get busy with something else and forget it. Other things, though, I just hate to toss away."

"It's awfully hot up here," Mel said, sitting down on a box to catch her breath. "We don't want Elvira to have to carry us out of here."

The grandmother said, "There's an echo of Clare up here." She opened a trunk full of old clothes and more quilts.

"Oh, I remember that," Mel said, looking at something in there.

I went to a shelf with some old metal toys, most of them broken, but curiosities all the same. There was a box labeled BOOKS at my feet, and I went through that. They looked like small encyclopedias, but when I opened them, I found they were medical books.

"Who did these belong to?"

"Your grandfather," the grandmother said, coming over to look at the one in my lap. "He worked for a year to be able to buy that set. He couldn't take me anywhere but for walks. He wanted to be a doctor back then."

"What happened?"

"We got married, and then your mother came along soon after. But he kept reading those books, his whole life long."

"Do you think he was disappointed he never got to be a doctor?"

"I doubt it," she said. "He was proud of his daughters."

"Oh, Momma!" Mel sat back, dragging a long swath of white something into her lap. "Is this your christening dress?"

"I am old, Melisande, but I am not that old. That would likely be your great-grandmother's christening dress. Possibly my mother's as well."

"Could I use it for this baby?"

"Why, of course," the grandmother said. The grandmother went back toward Mel. I stayed where I was, cool cloth pressed to the side of my face, looking at a long list of ailments.

"Oh, looky there. The crib is behind all that mess of dining room furniture I replaced when you and Clare were girls. So dark and heavy, this stuff. Like a lingering illness."

"Momma!" Mel peered into the shadowy space. "To anybody else's eyes, these are antiques."

"Elvira, child, help me here?" the grandmother asked. "I don't want your mother lifting things."

"Leave it till Clare can help her, Momma," Mel said.

"We'll just get it out here where we can see it."

"I've sidetracked us," Mel said. "You wanted to get that window painted."

"Tomorrow's another day," the grandmother said.

"Be careful, though, won't you?" Mel said. But she had already opened another trunk. "Oh, Momma. White cotton nightgowns. Would you look at all these tiny pleats? Can I take some of these?" Mel said. She began to rummage through that trunk of old white cotton things.

"Whatever you like."

Together, the grandmother and I moved the old furniture out of the way and carried the crib to the stairs, piece by piece, some wood, some metal. The pieces were surprisingly heavy, but we both pretended otherwise.

We stood back from the crib, wreathed in dust, a little breathless but happy to admire it. An old-fashioned picture of a fawn had been painted on each end.

"Look at that, hand-painted," Mel said, letting things fall back into the trunk. The grandmother reached out to help her get up. "It's beautiful, Momma."

But the grandmother said, "What's that I smell?"

We all sniffed.

"My lands, I've set the house afire again," she said, starting down the stairs at a run.

Chapter 22

I WAS right behind her, leaving Mel to bring up the rear, and I for one thought the grandmother was right. There was a definite smell of smoke as we headed for the first floor. And a kind of haze in the air in the kitchen; I could see it as we raced along the hall.

"Oh!" the grandmother cried, momentarily putting her hands up like she was being robbed. She hurried to the stove and turned off the fire under the teapot.

On the stove, the water had boiled away and the pot melted down—and more or less collapsed in on itself, was my best guess. The top was still the silvery pot color and shaped like a Hershey's Kiss, but the lower half of it was so hot it glowed red like a burning coal.

"Wow," I said.

"I put on a little water to make more iced tea while I was down here," Mel said, coming to a panting halt. "I thought we'd find that crib and come right back downstairs."

"It's not all that serious," the grandmother said. "Nothing's caught fire."

Mel said, "Why did you think it was your fault, Momma? You didn't leave anything on the stove."

"I thought maybe I did and forgot about it."

"If you had, Momma, it would only mean you got distracted like I did," Mel said.

"Out of sight, out of mind, as my mother used to say," the grandmother said.

"Come away from it. We can't do anything about it until it cools, anyway," Mel said, her paranoia about cooking appliances coming to the fore. "I don't think we ought to stand anywhere near it, in case it explodes or something."

"I'm sure I have a jar of instant iced tea in the pantry," the grandmother said. "Let's stir some up and sit outside."

An hour later, the Kiss no longer glowed red. The kitchen was still hazy with smoke. The grandmother said, "We ought to start up the exhaust fan in the attic. I wish I'd thought of it earlier."

Mel got a wooden spoon to take a gingerly poke at the Kiss. "It's welded onto the burner," she said. "And the burner is stuck to the stove."

"Let's find out if it's cool," the grandmother said. She put her fingers under the water tap and flung a few drops against the melted pot—they sizzled and dried away.

Mel said, "Momma! Don't make it mad," and made us all laugh.

The grandmother grabbed it with pot holders, but she couldn't jiggle the thing and said, "It's a permanent fixture."

Mel had looked under the sink and found a hammer. "Stand back," she said, and came at the Kiss swinging. She banged on it three or four times, knocking it every which way, but the Kiss didn't budge.

The noise rang through the room. I felt like I ought to be the one doing this, but from the first hit, my head started to hurt something awful.

The grandmother stepped in, saying to Mel, "Give that to me. You shouldn't be doing that in your condition." She gave the pot one good whack. There was a shriek of metal and suddenly the Kiss shot across the kitchen, hit the wall, and landed on a countertop, pretty as you please.

"My lands," the grandmother said, running her hand over the dent in the wall. "Did you see that thing go?"

"Look," I said. "Some of the pot stuck to the burner." I reached out to touch the slivers and drew back quickly to suck on my finger. "Sharp," I warned.

"I guess so," Mel said, inspecting the burner carefully. "Sword Making 101, Momma. Our Viking forebears would be proud of us."

The grandmother did seem strangely pleased, as if she

hadn't realized Mel was kidding. "A few more whacks with the hammer ought to break those pieces off," she said. "Help Elvira put a Band-Aid on that cut. You'll find them in the medicine cabinet back there."

And with that, the grandmother raised the hammer and whacked away at that burner, still firmly attached to the stovetop. I ran for the bathroom, eager to get out of the way of flying stove burners. To say nothing of how badly I needed more aspirin.

That's when we heard the all-too-familiar "Yoooo-hoo."

The grandmother ceased whacking.

Kerrie came in the door first, trying to slurp something bright green through a straw, and spotted the grandmother with the hammer. She halted, wide-eyed, making Aunt Clare practically fall over her.

The momentary silence was followed by a shrill "What in the world? Momma, what have you done?"

I said, "Mel let a pot boil dry."

"What is that?" Aunt Clare pointed to the silver lump on the counter.

"That's the pot," Mel said.

Aunt Clare finished a slow inspection of the premises and, in some way, of us. We each of us glanced around as she did this, but it seemed wrong to laugh; there was no chance of Aunt Clare finding anything funny in this.

"You all look so untidy," Aunt Clare said finally, and settled her glance on me. "Is that blood? Are you bleeding?"

I said, "It's just a little cut." A drop of blood fell on the floor.

"What have you all been up to? Apart from rendering the cooking pots unrecognizable, that is."

"We found a crib for the baby," the grandmother said.

Mel added, "In the attic. There's a christening dress too."

"I see," Aunt Clare said, much as if we'd spent the last hours lolling in the recliner while she built a new shopping mall with toothpicks and a hot-glue gun. She moved to set two department store shopping bags on the table in the alcove.

Mel eyeballed Kerrie. "What is that you're drinking?"

Kerrie shrugged as Mel moved toward her, and held the bottle out to be taken away.

Aunt Clare said, "She declared a thirst emergency on the way home."

Mel said, "This is one of those workout drinks. It's loaded with caffeine."

"I don't know," Aunt Clare said, taking the bottle in hand. "Is it? It's green. I figured it for some kind of soda."

"Clare, didn't you even look?"

"No, I did not. Don't make it sound like I tried to poison the child, Melisande. It's only caffeine."

Mel handed the bottle to me. "Pour it down the toilet, Elvira."

Aunt Clare looked at the grandmother and said, "Do you hear how she talks to me?"

"I'm just grateful the straw was too short for the bottle," Mel said. "If she drank it all, she'd probably go off like a rocket."

On my way to the bathroom, I could follow the grandmother's efforts to referee. "Don't appeal to me like you're four years old, either one of you," she said. "You are both grown girls. Don't hope for me to take sides later, when you get me alone. I'm an old woman who needs her peace and quiet."

Aunt Clare said, "Thank you, Momma, for making us feel like you're caught between a black widow spider and a tarantula."

"Don't expect to pick a fight with me either," the grandmother said. "I'll send you both home to your house, Clare. I'll let the grandchildren stay here where there is not a war going on, of course."

Once in the bathroom, I could hear their voices, but not clearly enough to follow the continuing battle. I was thinking, as I poured the green rocket fuel down the toilet, the grandmother knew her stuff. If family fights had loose corners, she pretty much nailed them all down.

"Don't flush, I'm going to tinkle," Kerrie said as she came into the bathroom.

"It might be dangerous to tinkle on caffeine," I said, in no mood to put up with any little-sister crap, even if this little sister wasn't yet guilty of any major offenses today.

"Then I'll pee on it," she said. "What's all the fuss about? Mel lets me have caffeine."

I held up the bottle. "Not half a gallon at a time."

"Sixteen ounces is not half a gallon," Kerrie said, but since she didn't take this point any further, I figured she wasn't all that sure. I got a Band-Aid, but no aspirin.

Kerrie said, "Here, I'll put it on for you."

"I got it." I shut the medicine chest and leaned my forehead against the mirror while I let the tap water run over the cut. "I'm beginning to understand why Mel stayed away from home all these years."

"Her mother?" Kerrie asked.

"Her sister."

"Is it about the dog?" Kerrie slid into the baby voice. "I miss Hound. I need a dog so much."

"It's just us here," I said, feeling suddenly like I just wanted to go to bed and maybe not get up again until tomorrow morning. "Stop talking like such a baby."

"Pregnancy is easy for you," she said in a surprising switch to her big-girl voice. The voice that drives me crazy. "You got Daddy."

"What do you mean?" But I knew what she meant. I really did.

Maybe it wasn't about favorites exactly, the way Aunt Clare thought, but I played guitar with Daddy, Mel took Kerrie to gymnastics. Daddy quizzed me when I had a big test coming up, Mel kept an eye on Kerrie's homework.

It probably started when Kerrie was a baby and Daddy took charge of getting me across the street safely. He took me out when the baby was napping. Pretty soon, when

Daddy went out to a flea market, or even to kick tires, he let me go along.

And that was fine with me. Because shopping for a car was interesting. A person took a drive. It was all about getting the best mileage and looking at leather interiors. I didn't want to stand around while Mel tried on twenty outfits and worried if her butt was too big.

"I'm not the baby anymore. I'm stuck in the middle now," Kerrie said, dropping the big-girl voice as well as the baby act. For the moment she was just herself, which might have been why I suddenly felt like talking to her.

"You aren't the only one with this problem, you know," I said. "American families have two point five children." I wasn't sure where I'd heard this. "There are plenty of families with middle kids."

"Yeah, we're the invisible ones." She'd heard a few news reports herself. "The point five, most likely."

"I'll share Daddy with you."

"Thanks, but I don't like flea markets all that much," Kerrie said. "And I don't want to help weed our garden."

I was sort of glad she had turned down this offer. I liked it that I got Daddy. Even if it meant that Mel and Kerrie didn't want him all that much sometimes.

Kerrie said, "I want that dog, and I want you to want her too."

At just that moment, Aunt Clare went rapidly past the bathroom on her way out and let the screen door slam behind her.

Chapter 23

KERRIE AND I went back to the kitchen in time to hear Mel slogging to the top of the stairs. The grandmother said, "I can make canned soup, if you girls like tomato rice or bean with bacon."

I thought maybe we ought to leave the stovetop alone, just for Mel's sake. "I'd be happy with leftover chocolate donuts, if that's okay with you."

"It's not," the grandmother said. "Not tonight, anyway. We just got through an upset over a caffeinated drink."

Good point.

"Mel lets us have peanut butter and jelly on Saturday night," Kerrie said. "We missed it this week."

"PB and J it is," the grandmother said. "So what's in the sacks?"

"We brought Elvira a get-well present," Kerrie said, and pulled it out of a bag. It was a T-shirt in swirly greens, with loose ruffly fabric where the sleeves ought to be. It had an allover shine, like glitter had been sprinkled on it.

It wasn't only the shirt; I couldn't accept a gift from Aunt Clare. "I don't think—"

"Oh, go on," the grandmother said. "If we all start taking sides over that drink, the fight will go on forever. Or until you go home, anyway."

Kerrie said, "It's just that Elvira hates green clothes. Aunt Clare and I meant to make that a joke, but now it seems kind of stupid. The T-shirt is for me. The CD player is for Elvira."

"CD player?" I looked in the other shopping bag and, sure enough, there was one. Plus two CDs. It still didn't seem quite right. "I got a CD player and you got a T-shirt?"

"We share the CD player when we get back home and you have your iPod back."

Which meant I got the loan of Kerrie's CD player now. "You are the queen of finagle," I said to her, which is what Daddy sometimes says to me. It's almost complimentary, the way he says it.

Kerrie said, "Is Finagle in Ireland?"

I said, "It means you got us both what we wanted."

Kerrie nodded, satisfied.

"Dinner is served," the grandmother said, setting three flavors of jelly beside the jar of peanut butter.

By the time we finished making sandwiches, Mel had

come back down, having changed out of her skirt and into stretch pants. She'd been crying. "Deal me in," she said as I put two slices of bread on a plate.

Over supper, Mel and the grandmother decided to watch a movie on TV. Kerrie and I were left behind to clean up, which was no big deal.

As I put away the peanut butter and jelly, I said, "I know this is probably the wrong time to bring this up again. But, Kerrie—"

"I know. We don't have room for the dog."

"Not that dog, anyway. Hound was heavy, but he was short. He was small."

"Okay."

This speedy agreement surprised me. After a moment, I said, "That's not the biggest problem we have."

I didn't mean Daddy.

Kerrie liked Aunt Clare. Having to choose between her and the grandmother would be much harder than being the middle sister.

She said, "Don't tell me the rest of it, okay?"

"Only because you let me rest my head in your lap."

"I also bought you aspirin," she said as she rinsed off our plates.

"You're on the verge of ruining this generous mood I'm in."

"I'll take my chances," she said on her way out of the kitchen.

I wiped the table, dropped the sponge on the drainboard, and followed the sound of a cheery argument. Mel and the grandmother couldn't decide which movie to watch: the old one just starting that everybody had seen or the new one that was already some ways into the story and nobody knew what was going on.

My ear weighed ten pounds and hurt hurt hurt. I felt like I was getting a fever, not that I cared to mention it. I settled into a wing chair so I could rest my head.

Kerrie was still awake when Mel woke me up. "Elvira, go up to bed."

The late news was ending. I'd been in that chair for hours. Like a zombie, I went to the kitchen and put batteries into the CD player.

I couldn't really wear the earphones. My ear was too sore. But I found I could hear just as well if I set them over my cheekbones. I didn't even have to turn up the sound. Weird, but fine, really.

Maybe Kerrie stayed up later. Maybe they all did. I was the only one making the trip upstairs. I thought my headache was a little better, but even if it wasn't, I intended to take full advantage of having a room to myself.

I picked out a book, I stacked up pillows to lean on. Since I'd already had a nap, I figured I wasn't likely to fade as fast as the night before.

As I pulled the quilt over myself, I glanced around the grandmother's sister's room. Golden eyes were looking right back at me. The grandmother's cat sat on the top of an armoire in the Egyptian statue pose. It was rusty-colored, like a marmalade cat mixed with a lot of brown.

"Here, kitty, kitty," I said after a moment.

It didn't flick a whisker.

I was tempted to try to stare it down, but I was too tired to win the contest. "I hope you're not going to keep me awake with eyes that glow in the dark," I said.

I didn't know I had fallen asleep again until Mel came in, gently slid the earphones off my face, and flicked my hair away from my ear. Before I went back to sleep, I added to the list I hadn't yet written into my diary.

Find out what makes cats purr.

Tomorrow, swab my ear with alcohol. If I could touch it at all.

Imagine what it would be like to sleep in this room more often. Which led to wondering what would have to happen to make that possible. Which led to thinking about Mel and Daddy. I thought about how for years they talked about moving back here.

Not that they talked to me about it. But sometimes, after I'd been put to bed and they thought I was sleeping, I would hear them sitting at the kitchen table, talking. Daydreaming, in a way. I never for a moment expected them to go anywhere.

Maybe Mel had some hopes, though. Because when Daddy stopped wanting to talk about moving back to Memphis and talked instead about making his comeback, she wasn't happy.

I fell asleep to the low sound of a cat motor.

Chapter 24

KERRIE WOKE sometime in the night, screaming bloody murder. I leaped out of bed, snatching the CD player and earphones off the bed table.

Mel and I nearly knocked each other over in the hallway. For me, it was just habit to react fast to this cry. Mel hardly knew what was going on. She switched on the overhead light in Kerrie's room.

Kerrie was sitting up in bed crying, shivering like all her dreams were horror movies. The sudden bright light didn't help any of us.

"Sweetie, what is it?" Mel asked her, squinting hard as she gathered as much of Kerrie onto her lap as possible. That left a lot of Kerrie hanging over onto the bed. I turned off the light. "What are you doing?" Mel asked as I put the earphones on Kerrie's head.

"We have to play the radio when she wakes up like this," I said. "Only there's no radio in here."

Mel looked confused. "You make it sound like this is something she does a lot."

"Not a lot. I usually wake up before she gets really into it. I turn on the radio and she falls asleep again right away. It happens when she worries about things." Even in the dark, I could feel Mel's anxiety. "Not that eight-year-olds usually worry about the things normal people worry about."

"I never realized," Mel said.

"You and Daddy sleep like the dead," I said. "Besides, your bedroom is on the other side of the house. I'm two feet away from her."

"You're a good sister," Mel said.

"Don't rely on it," I said, taking full advantage of Mel in a weak moment. "When the Belly is ready to move out of your room, I'm moving into your work shed. You and your furniture projects get the carport."

Kerrie had meanwhile slumped over the Belly, already quieting. Drugged by the music. I was glad I hadn't worn the batteries down. Together, we got her stretched out and threaded one arm through the earphone wires so she couldn't strangle herself. I could hear the music coming on strong, and I moved the earphones onto her cheekbones.

"What would she have to worry about?" Mel whispered as

we stood in the doorway and looked at Kerrie. In a shaft of moonlight we saw her eyelids spring open, then lower again.

"She wouldn't worry about Daddy going off to Las Vegas, do you think?" I felt a surly mood coming on. "Nah," I said, answering myself.

Mel pulled me out into the hallway, whispering, "She knows he'll come back."

"No, she doesn't, and neither do I," I said, keeping my voice low. "He went off on Friday. He drove to the airport and flew. Mel, he must've been in Las Vegas by the time you made popcorn."

Daddy should have called Saturday morning, the latest. I was mad now, seriously mad. If Mel tried to get in a word, I didn't know about it.

I said, "We still hadn't heard from him when we left on Sunday. By then he could have called at least twenty times, just figuring how many pay phones he must've walked past."

"Families go through things," Mel said. "That's all."

"There's a name for when families go through this," I said, "and it isn't 'that's all.'"

Mel said, "He was mad, okay, but I was mad too, and I'm over it. He's over it by now, and he'll come home, you'll see."

"Set it to music," I said. "Maybe you can sell it."

"You have a terrible mouth on you," Mel said, forgetting to whisper.

"Wonder where I get that."

"I'm serious, Elvira."

"You talk like you and Daddy are sharing a private

joke," I said. "Only Kerrie and I aren't in on it, and frankly, I don't think it's funny."

Mel put her fists on her hips. I could see her silhouetted in the little bit of light we had from the window in Kerrie's room. "Is that so?"

"Kerrie deserves better, and so does this one," I said, waving my hand in the general direction of the Belly. "They deserve exactly what you ask of me," I said. "Grown-up behavior."

"Is everything all right up there?" the grandmother asked from down below.

"We're fine, Momma," Mel said. "Kerrie had a little nightmare, is all."

"I don't think there's such a thing as a *little* nightmare," I said.

I went back to the grandmother's sister's bedroom—my bedroom—and shut the door. My night was wrecked. I didn't think Mel would go back to sleep either. Because Daddy could like Las Vegas better than New Hope. He might like looking like Elvis a whole lot better than a fired landscaper, even a fired and rehired landscaper.

Sure, Kerrie worried, but she slept through the worst of their big blowout. She didn't hear Daddy saying he thought Mel would rather see him holding a shovel than a guitar any day and getting pregnant was just one way of making that happen.

And Mel had said, "If you believe that, you should take your guitar and your shovel to Las Vegas and stay there."

"I just might do that," Daddy'd said. "I can be a land-scaper anywhere, but there isn't much use for my guitar here."

This was the sad truth.

I heard a small motor sound that I realized after a moment was the cat. I looked for it, but it was out of sight completely. Mel opened the door and, after standing there in the darkness for a minute, said, "What is that sound?"

"The cat." It sounded louder with the light out. "It doesn't seem friendly."

"Elvira, I want to order you not to worry, but I know that won't work."

"What will we do if he stays away and never calls?"

"He's coming home! Have you got that?" Mel said in a low, intense voice. "How can you think he wouldn't come home?" She sat down on the end of the bed. "I hope you won't tell Momma you're worried about such a thing. I don't want to have this talk with her. Or worse, with Clare."

"Because they won't know if he'll come home either?"

"Because it wouldn't be fair to your daddy to give them one more thing to hold against him."

"I don't get it," I said. "You're really not worried he won't come back? Plus, you decided you're okay with it if he wins. And deep down, you didn't really want to go along with him. Did you just not want him to have a good time?"

"Well, of course I want your daddy to have a good time." I could hear the surprise in her voice. "But I wanted him to have it with me. Even if I do look like a toad. I wanted him to rather stay with me if I didn't really want to go. Especially since I look like a toad."

"You don't look like a toad." She looked like the Goodyear blimp. I couldn't even imagine what she'd look like in two months.

Mel said, "Don't kid a kidder."

"A little bloated, maybe. But not a toad."

"If you think flattery is going to get you forgiven one minute before I stop wanting to lock you in a closet, you can just forget it."

But I knew that in some way, she didn't want to lock me up much.

"It's hard to explain feelings, Elvira. Especially when they don't all fit together the way we think they should. But feelings change, usually for the better somehow."

Chapter 25

WHEN I woke up early the next morning, my ear didn't feel like I'd hung a backpack from it. It was swollen, but not as bad as the day before. It was tender, but it didn't throb. My head didn't pound. I didn't have to walk tilted to one side.

All in all, I suspected I'd live.

I looked into the other bedrooms. Kerrie was sleeping, Mel was sleeping. But I could hear the grandmother moving around downstairs.

I knew I'd be putting a coat of paint on that window, so I dressed in a fairly new T-shirt that I didn't treasure. It couldn't impress the grandmother less than the Jimi Hendrix shirt.

She glanced at me as I went into the kitchen, then

looked back at her measuring cup. "I thought I'd make some hotcakes and we can just leave them in a warm oven. Let everybody eat as they get up and about."

"Sounds good to me," I said, following the smell of coffee. "What should I do to help?"

"You can explain to me how it is that your momma doesn't mind that you drink coffee but she had a conniption fit over that green soda."

"Mel has a twelve-year rule. Once I was twelve, I could drink coffee, smoke cigarettes if I wanted to kill myself, and drive." I remembered to add, "In the driveway."

The grandmother didn't look like this rested easy with her.

"Mel knew I wouldn't smoke, I hate the smell. So basically, she was saying I could drink coffee if I wanted to have something most kids couldn't have. Everything else, I have to wait till I'm twenty-four."

"What everything else was she worried about?"

"Boys."

The grandmother got a kick out of that. I was just thinking we were getting off to a good start, for six o'clock in the morning, when somebody knocked on the back door. I figured it was Aunt Clare making a sneak attack, and I opened the door with an oh-it's-you-again expression on my face.

It was Mr. Singer. Different colors today.

"Hello, Vertie," he said to the grandmother as he passed her a bucket about half filled with blueberries. She wasn't decorated with tissue paper this morning. She'd done her seven minutes before I got up.

He went on, saying, "I started picking and I just couldn't stop. I'd love a piece of that coffee cake you make."

The grandmother made all the grateful noises, but she looked a little perturbed. "I'd ask you in," she told him, "but I have to make the most of an opportunity to weasel all the family secrets out of this child. You understand."

Mr. Singer grinned and in a stage whisper said, "Bribery is helpful in these situations. Bribery and flattery."

"You may have something there," the grandmother said.

I felt pretty good as we shut the door. I had the grandmother to myself. I tried to strike just the right note. "You going to do some more banging on that burner?"

"No. There's just those clinging bits left on it. We'll do the hotcakes on that burner. The metal will soften up again. I'll push some strips of aluminum foil under it to catch any drips. But the window is more important to me right now. Do you think you could put a first coat on it this morning?"

"No problem."

We stuck to safe subjects while I ate, like my friend Debs and a roller-skating party. When the grandmother asked about Kerrie's ballet classes, I described her as a girl of quickly changing interests. An explorer.

The grandmother set the second plate of hotcakes into the warmed-up oven. She turned the oven off, though, and put the frying pan into the sink.

"Aren't you going to sit down to eat?" I asked.

She said, "I ate toast and a poached egg while I was making coffee. I don't have much of a sit-down habit. Are you ready to work?"

The grandmother opened the paint can while I made fast work of the dishes. "The brush may seem a little small for the job," the grandmother said as I climbed up on the counter. She made a show of barely dipping the brush and then scraping it against the edge of the can.

"A big brush would slap too much paint on at one time," she said. "Do around the glass first, while you have paint only on the tip of the brush. Then do the edges close to the wall."

I said, "I'll be careful."

"Throw this over your shoulder," she said, passing me a small damp cloth. It was thin as a hankie. "You have to wipe the paint off the window glass before it dries."

I said, "Where'd you learn so much about this?"

"Your grandfather was a housepainter," she said.

"A housepainter instead of a doctor."

"It suited him. Gave him lots of time to think. And now and then, if his day was hard, if the sun was hot or it rained unexpectedly, he came home and said he didn't lose any patients."

I painted about three inches along the edge before I got a dab of paint on the glass. Right away I used the little rag to wipe it off. "Don't get nervous," the grandmother said. "That happens to everybody. That's why I gave you the cloth."

When I needed more paint, she dipped and scraped and gave me the brush. She stood below me and supervised, but she didn't need to. I had made up my mind. I would paint this perfect window and all would be forgiven.

As I handed her the brush again, I asked, "Are you very religious or something?"

She glanced at me, then put more paint on the brush. "Why do you ask?"

"Well, Mel's never said one way or the other." I painted another three inches without screwing up. "About you, I mean. But she's not. We're not."

"Are you asking if this is a family trait?"

"No."

"So what are you working up to?"

"I noticed you don't really look at me. I wonder if it's a religious issue. If I'm 'an offense to thine eyes' or something."

"Not at all," she said as I dipped the brush myself. Still not meeting my eyes, but giving an approving nod as I scraped the brush, she added, "You're a very pretty girl, I think. And even if you end up with a cauliflower ear, you'll pass muster."

I didn't want her to think I was fishing for compliments, so I dove right in. "I can't help that Mel and Daddy didn't get married right away, you know."

"I know that."

As I stood up, paint dripped off my perfectly scraped

brush. But she was ready with a damp sponge and wiped it up.

"This is the twenty-first century," I said. "We don't brand red *A*'s on people's foreheads anymore, and illegitimate children aren't suspected to be the spawn of the devil."

"Quite a history buff, are you?" she asked me.

"Kerrie is the history buff. But I read."

"So did my sister."

"I didn't know you had a sister," I said, and blopped paint on the glass. Blopped and wiped. "I mean, I know I'm in her room, but I hadn't heard of her until yesterday."

"She died when she was just about your age," the grandmother said. "Pneumonia. You look so much like her, I was afraid of staring."

I dipped and scraped. "You miss her a lot?"

"I didn't realize how much until I saw your face," she said. "I'll show you some pictures later, if you like."

"I don't mind if you stare."

She wrapped her hand around my ankle in a way that was strangely comforting. "You're not illegitimate. Your mother is married to your father."

"Not until after I was born." Not until only a few days before Kerrie was born.

"That's just a technicality," she said.

We were both quiet for a minute. My painting arm had stopped of its own accord. I asked her, "Does this paint make your eyes burn? It sure does make my eyes burn."

She patted me on the foot.

"Can I call you Grandma?"

She gave me one of her sharp looks. "You call your mother Mel, you want to call me Grandma?"

"How about Granny? Or Grammie, that would be really cu—"

"Grandma will be fine," she said in a dry tone.

My painting arm had gone back to work. I could have called her Grandma right off to get the ball rolling, but I didn't want to do that. I wanted to wait for the right moment. It was like waiting for Christmas.

"I'm going to put some paint in a jar for you," the grandmother said. "So you don't have to keep bending over to the can all the time."

"Thanks."

"It'll cut down on the dripping."

Hmmm. Message decoded: "Don't drip paint all over the place."

Mel came downstairs about twenty minutes later.

"The paint smell woke me," she said. "I see you dressed for dirty work."

"These are my clothes," I said. Crabby is what Mel gets when her stomach is about to turn over.

"I'm going to put on some water for tea," she said.

"Don't turn on the gas," the grandmother said in an alarmed voice. "You should never start a fire where there are paint fumes in the air."

"It won't explode in here, Momma," Mel said in a falsely understanding voice.

"I'm not worried about a fire," the grandmother said testily. "But it makes a terrible odor, and I can't believe it's healthy to breathe that odor in."

Mel got a Coke from the fridge, sighing pretty much the same deep sigh she hated for me to sigh when she was giving orders.

"That isn't the right breakfast for a woman in your condition," the grandmother said.

"I agree," Mel said. "But I'm going to go sit outside and drink it."

"There's hotcakes in the oven," the grandmother said.

"In a while," Mel said. "I don't know that I could hold it down just this minute." She, lucky woman, went out the door as Aunt Clare came in.

"Well, good morning to you too," Aunt Clare muttered to herself.

"Mel never quite got over the morning sickness thing," I said. "The doctor says it's about a nerve getting pressed on."

"I'll make up a plate for her," the grandmother said, pulling a cookie sheet out of the oven. "Hotcakes ought to go down easy when she's ready. Clare, come stand next to Elvira. And don't turn on the gas, either one of you."

"How are you feeling, darlin'?" Aunt Clare said.

It took a moment to realize she meant me. "It's not so

bad. Thank you, Aunt Clare, for the CD player. Thanks for thinking of me."

"You're welcome. I thought a charm bracelet might be nicer, but Kerrie was sure the CD player was a better bet."

The grandmother went out the back door, carrying plates—hotcakes stacked on the top plate—syrup, forks, and napkins, like a professional.

"I'm not going to fall off here, you don't have to worry."

"I'm not worried. Momma's worried." Aunt Clare reached for a hotcake, rolled it up like a cigar, and started to eat. "Where's Kerrie?"

"Still sleeping."

"You and I haven't exactly hit it off," she said. "Why is that?"

I stopped painting and looked down at her. "You're a little hard on Mel, that's why."

"That's between sisters," Aunt Clare said. "I'm asking about you and me."

"Sisters have to be able to count on each other," I said.

"I agree," Aunt Clare said. "So while you may not like everything you see and hear when I'm around, maybe you could remind yourself I need my sister now. I think Momma needs her too."

"I'll keep that in mind." I shoved the window open so I could paint around the bottom without bending over to it.

"You know, I think I'll go sit in the garden too," Aunt Clare said. "If that paint smell makes you dizzy in the least, get down from there and come outside with us."

She went out the back door, and the kitchen was quiet again.

I heard Mel say, "I used to dream about raising my children in this house, Momma. Of course, that was before I had any, but still, I'd hate to see you sell it."

Mel was sitting beneath the window, the grandmother beside her.

"You know, it's not too late to bring your family back here."

"Tony and I used to talk about moving to Memphis, Momma."

"And now?"

"Now we talk about other things."

"Yoo-hoo, don't say anything you wouldn't want me to hear," Aunt Clare called, coming around the corner of the house.

The chairs were shifted a little, and when Aunt Clare sat down, they all agreed it was going to be a hot day. For about a minute nobody said anything.

Then the grandmother said, "I didn't expect to tell the both of you together, but I'm glad it's worked out Mel's here. Mr. Singer has asked me to marry him. I've said yes."

Both Mel and Aunt Clare whooped and made happy noises; it took a minute for me to sort out their voices.

Mel said, "When did this happen?"

"Last week."

Aunt Clare said, "And you haven't said a word till now?"

"I didn't want you to think I'd marry because you're

worried about me, Clare," the grandmother said. "I hope you girls don't believe I'm too old to remarry either."

"No, of course not," Aunt Clare said.

Mel added, "I'm not sure there is such a thing as being too old for love."

The grandmother said, "I know I said some harsh things when you left home so long ago, Melisande. Especially when you got pregnant."

"I know you didn't mean them, Momma."

"Of course I meant them. But I might have been wrong then. Certainly I'd be wrong now. Times have changed. Maybe they had already changed."

"Thank you, Momma."

"On a practical note, Mr. Singer's house is smaller than this one and, in some ways, more convenient," the grandmother said. "Better suited to old people."

"We'll help you do whatever you want to do," Aunt Clare said. "I mean, I know Mel can't stay away from home forever, but—"

"The baby's not due for two months," Mel said. "Only, I'll have to put the girls back in school before then."

"You might think again about moving back here," the grandmother said.

"Oh, Momma—"

"It's just something to think about," the grandmother said. "Well, let me take this breakfast plate over to Mr. Singer. His hotcakes will have to be heated up again."

I heard Kerrie moving around in Aunt Clare's old

room, and for a few minutes I let myself think about what it would be like to live in this house.

"Well, what do you think of that?" Aunt Clare said after the grandmother had gone out of sight around the hedge.

"He's a sweetie," Mel said. "I'm wondering how you'd feel if Tony and I ever moved back here. Would we mean the end of your social life?"

"You were right. I'm not a cheerleader anymore," Aunt Clare said. "I should never have said that."

"Things we should never have said seem to run in this family. How would you feel about us living nearby? Not that I know if that's even possible. Tony would have to want to."

"I hope you will, Melisande. I hope you can."

"If there's any real threat of it," Mel said, and I didn't have to see her smile to know it was there, "you'll be the first to know."

They got up and walked away. I slid the window down a little to make sure the drying paint didn't glue it in one spot. My fingertips were stiff with dried paint, and my shirt was ruined.

I noticed I was soaked with sweat, but for ten minutes or so, I had my thoughts to myself and nobody bothered me. It didn't take me that long to decide painting was boring. Still, I wanted to finish.

The back door opened again.

"I'm going to go peek in at Kerrie," Aunt Clare said, Mel coming right behind her. "I won't wake her."

I said, "We aren't worried." And got paint on the window glass as I looked at her.

Mel put her plate into the kitchen sink, saying, "I'm putting on water for tea and I'm going right back out."

"So the ban on not using the stove has been lifted?" I asked, wiping paint off the glass.

"No, but yesterday we were going through iced tea the way a herd of elephants takes up pond water," Mel said. "So I'm making tea now."

The funny thing was, the paint did smell worse only a minute after Mel turned on the gas. It wasn't so much the paint smell as the gas smell that seemed stronger. We wrinkled our noses at each other.

"Momma may be right." Mel turned off the fire. "We can make instant tea, I guess. Are you finished up there?"

"Nearly." Nearly finished with the hard part, anyway.

Kerrie started downstairs, with Aunt Clare right behind her, calling, "She was already awake, I swear."

"She was," I said. "I heard her walking around earlier."

"Where's your mother?" Kerrie asked Mel as she came into the kitchen.

"Call her your grandmother, please," Mel said.

"Your grandmother, please," Kerrie said.

"Hey!" Mel said.

"Grandma," I said loudly, and then, because I had their attention, added, "She agreed to that."

"You don't say." Mel broke into a big grin.

"I made a suggestion while we were painting the window."

"Grandma sounds fine to me," Mel said. "Kerrie?"

"Okay."

"There are blueberry hotcakes under a towel in the oven," Mel told her. "Do you want some?"

"Fine," Kerrie said, and sat down at the table.

"Here, here," Aunt Clare said, hopping into the middle of things. "You're a big enough girl to get your own hotcakes. Your momma can't be waiting on you hand and foot anymore."

"Fine, fine." Kerrie got up again and opened the oven door. She plucked out a pancake and held it like a slice of pizza for the first bite. Then she set it on the table without bothering to look for a plate. "Milk?"

"Fridge," Aunt Clare said, and pointed to a cabinet. "Glasses in there."

"Good," Mel said, "because the paint's too strong for me. Elvira, I want you down from there, whether you're finished or not. You need ventilation, and I am not talking about the holes in your ears."

I dipped, scraped, and painted a little faster. Paint dripped onto the towel. The grandmother came through the back door. "Mr. Singer has invited us all to dinner," she said.

"Grandma's getting married," I told Kerrie.

"Oh, Grandma," Kerrie said, hugging her around the waist.

"What do you feed this child?" the grandmother asked in a sorry attempt at a critical tone. "She is tiny. Surely we can remedy that."

Kerrie said, "I eat plenty," and bit into her pancake.

"I've got mouths to feed over at my place," Aunt Clare said, pouring milk into a small glass. "I came over to find out if the girls might like to help me. If it's all right with you, Mel."

Mel gave me a glance, but I hardened my heart.

"Pleeeeee-uz," Kerrie begged.

"No, thanks," I said. "I don't want to miss the puppy when I go home."

"What a sweet thing to say," Aunt Clare said, as if surprised. She handed the milk to Kerrie. "I thought maybe you didn't care for dogs."

"Both the girls loved Tony's old dog," Mel said. "You poked Elvira in a tender spot."

The grandmother said, "Elvira and I can attend to this window before the heat gets too bad. We want to bring that crib downstairs too."

"I'm coming along with you," Mel said as Kerrie guzzled her milk down. "I like puppies, you know."

"I like Mr. Singer," I said when the others had gone.

"I like him too. Old people need companionship. It's just icing on the cake that I love him a little bit."

"Just a little bit?" I asked, seeing her blush again.

"Now don't tease. You're old enough to fall in love yourself, but you don't know what a serious step this is for me."

"I bet I do."

"I bet," the grandmother said. "How often do you say 'I bet' in a week's time?"

I shrugged.

The grandmother said, "When you're young, you take chances. You take chances because you're counting on more chances."

"You have chances," I said. "Mel wanted another chance. And you opened the door. Maybe that's how it works."

"Maybe that's true."

"I'm giving you a chance," I said, "and you're giving me one."

"I'm getting very lucky all of a sudden," she said. "Maybe I shouldn't turn down any chances that come my way."

"That could be a song," I said.

Chapter 26

MEL AND Kerrie and Aunt Clare got back just about the time I finished with that window. Kerrie had stars in her eyes. "If we find a bigger house," she said, "we might have room for a baby *and* a puppy."

Which meant Mel had fallen in love with the puppies. I said, "I'm glad you kept a lid on it so you wouldn't get her hopes up."

"I know, I know," Mel said.

"Don't pick on your momma," Aunt Clare said.

I said, "You pick on yours." I was hot and sweaty enough to say whatever came to mind. No matter what the consequences.

To Mel, Aunt Clare said, "I have no doubt this is what comes of letting them call you by your first name."

"Don't you pick on me either," Mel said, and then turned to me. "That window looks finished."

"Close enough," I said. "But it gets another coat tomorrow, I think."

"Let's go bring that crib down," Aunt Clare said. She brushed at her slacks as if she'd found a little of our dust on them. I noticed then that she was dressed pretty much like a normal person. Not a bead in sight. However, she wasn't quite dressed for tackling the attic.

I said, "It needs some cleanup."

"Oh," she said. "Well. All right, then. We'll carry it outside and turn the hose on it."

Aunt Clare turned out to be better at taking on her share of the work than I thought she would be. We wrangled the four sides, some long metal rails, and the flat springs down the narrow attic stairs, and then out to the water spigot under the kitchen window. By then we had come to some kind of understanding about getting along.

Or maybe we were just too tired to spit.

Once we had everything in place, I said, "Stand back so you don't ruin your outfit."

While I scrubbed the crib with soap and water, she asked, "Are you looking forward to having a little baby in the house?"

"Oh, yeah, it's a dream come true," I said unenthusiastically.

"Oh. So you're not happy about this."

"I'm thirteen. Kerrie is eight. I don't know anyone who has a brother or sister under five."

"So you think they're too old," Aunt Clare said. "Mel and Tony?" The note of real regret in her voice brought me up short.

"It just seems that way to me," I said, thinking suddenly of what the grandmother said about her chances.

"That's what I want to know," Aunt Clare said. "How it seems to you."

Sadly, that was all the encouragement I needed.

"Parents are always making decisions that change kids' lives and we're supposed to go, 'Hey, that's okay,' every time. I saw this movie where the dad takes the whole family to Africa and they have to live like Robinson Crusoe. Then things go bad and they end up on a boat, either dying of thirst or getting half drowned. Mel and Daddy aren't that bad, of course. It's only a baby."

"Are you afraid things will go bad?"

One part of my mind was completely aware that Aunt Clare might very well be the worst possible person to confide in. Another part argued that I wouldn't ever be sure I could trust her until I tested her.

I said, "Daddy went off to that Elvis competition even though Mel wanted him to stay home."

"Didn't she want to go?"

It occurred to me that these were precisely the things Mel wouldn't have said to Aunt Clare, but I was on a kind of downhill slide, I couldn't stop myself.

I remembered Mel didn't want to make Daddy look bad. Probably she didn't want to look bad either. I said, "She wanted to go looking her best, I guess, the way Daddy did. So she stayed home."

"I can't imagine Mel being too happy about that."

I said, "She's always asking, 'Do I look too much like I swallowed a watermelon whole?' Like she could possibly have this baby without ever looking like that. Or she asks, 'Will you help me shave my legs if it gets to where I can't reach them?'"

"Well, that would be pretty horrible," Aunt Clare said. "Not to be able to reach around the watermelon, I mean. But I don't think it's very likely."

"I don't mind helping her shave her legs. But a few months from now it'll be, *I'm going to the store, take care of the baby. I feel like taking a nap, watch the baby. Your daddy and I are going to a movie, blah-de-blahblahblah*. Who asked me if I want to change diapers or feed the baby or get spit up on? There is a reason why I don't babysit for money."

My voice had gone higher and higher, until I heard it in my ears like a tape played at high speed. I took a deep breath and shut up.

"What *do* you do for money?" Aunt Clare asked in a problem-solving tone. "I mean, if you get an after-school job and maybe work on Saturdays, that keeps you out of the house for a while."

"I work for Daddy," I said, as if I was chained to a plow. But I could only hope that it was still true.

"Then you can plead homework," Aunt Clare said. "Get on the honor roll so they can't argue that either."

"That's an idea," I said, not believing for one minute that my troubles were over.

I could get on the honor roll—all that took was determination and giving up all my free time and never caring about all the fun I'd had as a B-minus student. And Mel would still expect me to babysit.

It was funny, though, how Aunt Clare had turned into somebody who was good to talk to. Then I realized we hadn't heard any of the others for a while. I said, "Where is everybody?"

"Momma's probably showing Mel Mr. Singer's garden," Aunt Clare said. "Some kudzu vine must've wrapped its tendrils around them." She brushed her hands through her hair, pushing it back from her sweaty face. She looked like a crazy woman. The kind that now and then gives good advice. "Grab a machete and let's go rescue them."

I followed her.

Chapter 27

MR. SINGER'S garden grew by leaps and bounds and grew half wild besides. It stretched from one corner of the yard to the other and crept close to the house at the sides.

In the center of the backyard, a waist-high cement sundial stood in a pea-gravel circle, with flowers scattered about wherever they had sprung up.

Mel was sitting in the gravel on a chair cushion, pulling weeds. Even Kerrie knew a weed when she saw one, thanks to Daddy's training. Most of the time, anyway. As we walked over there, Mel was looking at something limp and twisted beyond reviving. She said, "If you have any doubts, let the plant stand."

The grandmother pulled weeds from a deep well of

energy. That is, she started out weeding, but soon she was moving entire plants from one spot to another.

"Momma, this isn't even your garden," Aunt Clare scolded as she hurried to take the weight of the plant. "Not yet, anyway."

I waved to Mr. Singer, who could be seen at the window over his sink. He waved back.

"It's that time of year for dividing some and saving others," the grandmother was saying. "That work won't wait. Be careful now, you'll dirty your pants."

"Too late," Aunt Clare said, scurrying to hold up the business end of the shovel. Kerrie took hold too, and they all went around the corner of the house.

"She has only to pass a flower bed to set it quaking in fear," Mel said to me in a low voice. I figured she meant the grandmother, since Aunt Clare would be no threat to the flower beds.

I sat down to help with the weeding.

"I want your reaction to something," Mel said. "But only after you take a deep breath and answer back in a low voice."

"Shoot," I said, following a long strand of root to another sprouting of weeds.

"I think I want to bring us back here to live," she said. "I'm seriously considering it."

I looked at her from under my eyebrows.

"We'd have this big house," she said. "We can buy it

from Momma. She'll be living next door, so we can always look in on her and Mr. Singer as they get older."

"Are we talking Daddy too?"

"Of course I'm including your daddy."

"He's got his business to think about."

"He lost his three biggest customers for no good reason, may their roses get black spot and thrips," Mel said.

"He got them back."

"He's in the mood for a change," Mel said.

I said, "We haven't heard from Daddy. Does that still not bother you?"

"We aren't at home, and this is the last place he'd ever expect to find us. Can you just stop talking like he isn't coming back unless we get home and he still isn't there?"

Things had been rough lately, but until the competition rolled around and they had their big blowout, I had not worried about Daddy leaving us. So I pulled out a few timothy weeds, waiting to see if I could go along with Mel on this.

I said, "It's just that he looked so different, I guess. No, it's that he acted different. He was different."

Mel nodded. "Okay, he is different for the hours at a time that he's trying to channel Elvis. But I promise, once he wins this contest, you will not have to stare at a row of look-alike men and wonder which one is the real Tony Ruggiero. He'll be the one waving and grinning like a fool."

"What if he doesn't win?"

"Oh, he'll win," Mel said.

"That's the other thing," I said. "If he does win, doesn't Elvis come home to live with us? Don't get me wrong, it's amazing Daddy can do that. The Elvis thing, I mean. Cool, even. But I don't want Elvis for a dad. I want *my* dad."

"I know what you mean," Mel said. "All those years on the road, I had to practically walk tiptoe not to wake him too early in the morning, which was not easy for me when you were little, believe me."

I did believe her. I sort of remembered, just not clearly.

We pulled a few more weeds before she added, "It wasn't easy for you either. I used to worry it was like you were living with alcoholics or something, demanding that you be quiet and then making you put up with a lot of loud music when your daddy was working. I figured you were going to grow up confused."

I sat back on my heels. It was like hearing about a bad dream I had every so often, but forgot about in between.

"About once a month, we had to have this big fight that kind of knocked your daddy down to ordinary size again." Mel twisted the flowering head off a weed before she went on. "I had just about had it with him when I got pregnant with Kerrie. She saved our marriage, I think, because she forced us to get off the road."

"But Daddy's not like that now," I said.

"It wasn't till he took up gardening that I found out what a sweetie I was married to. The daddy you know is the man I love best. I don't want to go back to the old ways either."

"How can you make sure?"

"He's more grown-up now, Elvira," Mel said. "I know you think we fall short, but we're both more grown-up now."

We both fell to weeding with a ferocity we couldn't keep up in the heat. But it felt good for that two or three minutes that we did it.

"I heard you talking to Aunt Clare," Mel said. "I was close by the hedge and you were talking over the noise of the water."

"Yeah?" I said, like I'd said nothing of any great importance. But inside, my heart considered a swoon. I hadn't been in trouble for about fifteen running minutes, and it was beginning to feel good to me.

"I can hire a babysitter, you know. And if you feel so strongly about it, I won't expect you to change diapers."

I sighed. "We'll all help with the baby," I said. "Especially Kerrie. She's at that age where the baby's going to look like a big doll to her."

Mel didn't look convinced.

"The way she looked to me once or twice before she was two years old and into my stuff all the time. Of course, I thought she was *your* doll."

"So eight's a good age, is it?" Mel asked. "To find you have a baby in the house, I mean."

"It really is. Six years old was all wrong. I was just starting school, I thought I was being replaced."

"So what about thirteen?"

"I don't know yet. We'll probably just need to set limits."

"On what?"

"On how often you can say watch the baby. And for how long. Like that."

"That sounds reasonable."

I thought about living in Memphis. It didn't sound bad. We wouldn't have to start a new garden from scratch. Mr. Singer said there are some kids on the next block. One of them is a tall girl, he said, and I figured she might like having me around.

"I'll tell you a secret," I said. "Grandma has every picture of us you ever sent her. She's going to love having a grandbaby nearby."

"She already does," Mel said. "She isn't half so crabby as when we first showed up, is she?"

"Besides, she'll be over here soon enough," I said, looking around the garden. A lot of the best flowers were already done. But the border around the house was bright with the reds and yellows of August, attracting butterflies.

I pointed. "What are those little yellow ones called?"

"Butter stamps," Mel said.

"Really?"

She nodded. "Not scientifically, I guess. But that's what we always called them."

It seemed to me we could do with a little music on the air, but over our heads, a blue jay and a squirrel were having a big disagreement. Mel and I sat back and wondered what their problem could be.

Chapter 28

MR. SINGER came out of the house wearing oven mitts and carrying a casserole. "We're eating in your grandma's garden, where it's cooler," he said. "Why don't you come along and help me set things up?"

Like they heard the dinner bell, Aunt Clare and Kerrie came around the house. "Momma, come on, tell us what's broke and what's not," Aunt Clare called.

We pulled some wicker chairs and this cute little love seat out of the garage and washed our hands under the garden hose. Mel and Mr. Singer readied a table in the grandmother's garden. Inside of ten minutes we had settled ourselves.

"Your momma said you girls like macaroni and cheese," Mr. Singer said, "which just happens to be my specialty."

Well, it really truly was.

It was, on the whole, like a holiday where wars are stopped, at least temporarily. There was a breeze, so the bugs weren't bad. It was quiet, except for talk of gardens and things we'd found in the attic.

The grandmother told us what might be found in some of the other trunks and boxes. She looked happy, even though she had a smudge of dirt on her cheek and her hair had tumbled down at the back of her neck.

"I think we need ice cream," she said.

"I'll get it," I said.

"No, I'll get it," Mel said. "I'm saving you for the dishes."

Mr. Singer followed her into the house to help. I was picking up our plates when I noticed this car coming slowly down the street. Although it was getting dark, the car didn't have lights on, so it seemed the driver expected to stop soon. And because I looked, Aunt Clare looked.

The car pulled up in front of the house.

Kerrie was bent over some leafy pieces of ground cover that broke off during weeding and the grandmother had pulled from her pocket. "They'll take root in a few days, if we're careful to water them," she said. Then she and Kerrie heard the engine cut off and looked in that direction.

Daddy got out of the car, yet hung back, the way boys will. The streetlight flickered on and lit his white jacket with a ghostly glow.

After a couple of false starts toward us, he opened the

door to the backseat and took out his guitar. I smoothed my hair down to make sure the earrings were covered.

Mel pushed open the back screen door and looked out. She couldn't see Elvis. "We're dipping double strawberry and butter pecan. Anybody want chocolate syrup?"

"Daddy's coming," Kerrie said.

"He can't be." This was Mel. But her voice was already full of hope. Her face lit up and she came out to meet him.

That is, Mel came on outside and sat down on the back steps so she wouldn't look too anxious. I knew exactly how she felt. Only she still held the ice cream scoop. Kerrie got up and ran to do the greeting.

Elvis held his guitar in one hand and swept her up under the other arm, swinging her in a circle the way Daddy always does. I kept my seat beside the grandmother. I'm too big for that swinging stuff, anyway.

And then they came on, Kerrie pulling and pushing, impatient with Daddy's slow swagger. I had this big wrestling match going on in my heart, never knowing what I wanted: to get up and say hey, or to sit there and see what happened.

"How did you know to come here?" Mel asked as Kerrie pushed Daddy around the corner of the house. "You're supposed to be in Vegas through the weekend."

And he stopped there, not moving closer to anyone, with Kerrie dangling from the end of one arm and his guitar from the other. Maybe he was unsure of his welcome. Certainly I felt unsure.

The ice cream scoop dripped on Mel's foot, and she held it away, shook it. Then got up to wipe her foot sideways across the grass.

"I called home over and over. At first, when you didn't answer, I thought you were still mad. Maybe mad all over again that I waited till Sunday afternoon to call."

He looked ashamed of himself, the way my daddy would have been, but it was unconvincing in Elvis. "After a while, it worried me," he said. "I thought to call in and check the messages. When I heard your sister say your momma was dying, I knew you needed me."

I glanced over in time to see the grandmother give Aunt Clare a you-said-what? look. Aunt Clare pretended she was too caught up in Daddy's apology to notice.

"I can't believe you know how to call our machine for messages," Mel said, getting up to meet him.

"I do it practically every day, when you're in the greenhouse," Daddy said. "In case one of our girls needs to come home early from school or something."

"That's never happened," Mel said.

Too true. Kerrie and I hardly ever missed a day of school, let alone got sent home sick. Kerrie broke away from Daddy to turn cartwheels in the grass.

"Why, your momma hasn't aged a day," he said, and came over to us. He wore that easy walk that belonged to Tony Ruggiero. "How are you feeling, ma'am?"

"Reports of my death were greatly exaggerated," the grandmother said.

"I'm glad to hear that. What do you think of my little girls?"

"I'm pleased to meet them," the grandmother said. "You must be a good daddy to have raised such fine people."

"It was worth coming all this way to hear that," Daddy said.

Mr. Singer came out of the house carrying a tray filled with dishes of ice cream. He had one for Daddy too. There were introductions to be got through, and then conversation happened in dribs and drabs between bites.

Mel said, "When did you perform? When will they announce the winner?"

"I didn't get onstage," Daddy said. "You needed me, honey, so I came on home. Nothing else mattered."

"Oh, Tony." Mel looked miserable. "You missed your chance? I'm so sorry, I know you would've won."

"The only win that matters is right here," Daddy said.

This was echoed by answering sighs on the part of Aunt Clare and the grandmother.

"Do you mean you left early?" Mel asked, putting one hand to her head. "I've suddenly lost track of time. Could you go back and still be on time?"

"Who cares," he said, and laughed. And I almost knew him. Unless Elvis also laughed like that. I couldn't be sure. "This isn't going to make sense, but I used to dress up like Elvis to feel like me. Only now I do feel like me. Except when I dress up like Elvis."

"What do you mean?" Mel said. "Are you done with this?"

"When you've seen one Elvis, you've seen them all, isn't that what you told me before I left?"

"Oh, I was just mad at you." Mel looked a little embarrassed. Then she rallied, saying, "The truth is, you have never been more able to deliver that Elvis experience. I know that. More important, you know that."

Daddy shrugged. "I'm sorry for the way I left," he said. "I'm sorry I left at all. But I had to do it to know the truth of how things stood, I guess. I hope you can forgive me."

"I could try," Mel said with the smile that always let Daddy off the hook. It was still weird to see her smile that smile at Elvis, but I kept reminding myself that Daddy was in there somewhere.

He kissed Mel on the top of her head. "Miss me?" he asked her.

"I did. I knew there were good reasons to be married to you, even after you left mad," Mel said. "Even though I was mad at you too."

"Elvira, you haven't said hello," Daddy said, his arm still around Mel's shoulders.

"How long before that stuff comes out of your hair?"

"I'll wash it out tonight," he said. "It's not permanent."

"Good."

"Elvira wants her daddy back," Mel said.

"Elvis will never try to take your daddy's place," he said

to me. "See if you can't find a place in your heart for him, though. I'll sing you a song, if you like." Daddy lifted the guitar and noodled around on it for a few moments. Then Elvis began to sing.

"My lands," the grandmother said under her breath. She looked impressed. Aunt Clare looked like she was falling in love. I looked over at my mother, wanting to excuse myself and go into the house.

Mel was grinning, not impressed at all. She was looking at Daddy doing his Elvis act. That's what made it okay for me. I could watch him do his Elvis act too.

By the third song, I had to agree, he wasn't half bad. A yellow butterfly had come to hover in the air over him, probably drawn by the scent of Brylcreem.

"Love me tender, love me sweet, never let me go," Daddy sang, and the butterfly twirled overhead. "You have made my life complete, and I love you so."

When Daddy finished singing, I got up and hugged him. "I'm glad you're home," I said. Only once the words were out did I realize I meant the whole of us. We were home. When we were all together, we were home.

"I have to tell you," Daddy said to Mel as he handed me his guitar. "Las Vegas was a disappointment."

"How so?"

"You remember how often we've read that they cleaned Las Vegas up, that it's become a family entertainment mecca?"

"Yes."

"Well, that's all over. A few hours there and I knew it wasn't the place to raise our girls."

"No?"

"I swear, I saw a girl Elvira's age, Mel, just opened my eyes," Daddy said. "How long would it be before they'd be trotting around with glitter nail polish and a pierced something or other."

I put my hand up, realizing for the first time that my ear had stopped hurting. There was an odd silence, all of us digesting this turn in the conversation.

"No time at all," the grandmother commented.

Mel, who'd been the most silent of all, if such a thing is possible, laughed out loud.

"What's funny about that?" Daddy asked, standing before us in his black patent Elvis hair.

"Nothing until now, I swear," Mel said. "Come sit beside me, sweetheart, and let me tell you about our last few days."

Acknowledgments

SPECIAL JOYFUL thanks to Shana Corey, my editor, for recognizing the endearing qualities to be found under Elvira's spiky exterior, and to the team at Random House who supports us.

Very special thanks to Joanne Russell and Nicole de las Heras for their part in this one. It's just spectacular.

Still and always thanking my husband, Clark—uh, no, Akila—for reading, encouragement, and support. And for meals when I've used up every last particle of energy getting the words on the page.

Thank you to Susan, who read and encouraged and got Akila and me out of the house now and again for breakfasts at the donut shop and roofing projects and literary evenings at the local bistro, and to her daughter, Hannah, who read the manuscript all the way to the end in one weekend.

And my agent, Jill Grinberg, should know that the very thought of her causes Akila and me to do a little happy dance all around the house. I suspect I've said this before, but it's still true. Of course we thank her.

About the Author

AUDREY COULOUMBIS'S first book for children, *Getting Near to Baby*, won the Newbery Honor in 2000. She is also the author of several other highly acclaimed books for young readers, including *Say Yes*, an IRA Children's Book Award winner; *Summer's End*, a Book Sense 76 Pick; and *The Misadventures of Maude March*, a New York Public Library 100 Titles for Reading and Sharing Selection, a Book Sense 76 Pick, and a National Parenting Publications Gold Award winner. Audrey lives in upstate New York and Florida with her husband, Akila, and their dog, Phoebe. Audrey and Akila have two grown children. You can visit Audrey's Web site at www.audreycouloumbis.com.